Uncovering You 2: Submission

(Uncovering You, #2)

Scarlett Edwards

UNCOVERING YOU #2: SUBMISSION

Copyright © 2014 Edwards Publishing, Ltd.

Edited by Gail Lennon.
Cover design by Scarlett Edwards.
Interior design by Scarlett Edwards.

Published by Edwards Publishing, Ltd.

Edwards Publishing
477 Peace Portal Drive
Suite 107-154
Blaine, WA 98230

The uploading, scanning, and distribution of this book in any form or by any means---including but not limited to electronic, mechanical, photocopying, recording, or otherwise---without the permission of the copyright holder is illegal and punishable by law. Please purchase only authorized editions of this work, and do not participate in or encourage electronic piracy of copyrighted materials. Your support of the author's work is appreciated.

ISBN: 978-0-9937370-2-2

Uncovering You 2: Submission

by Scarlett Edwards

Edwards Publishing

Book Description:

I have survived the worst. I have come out of the darkness with my sanity intact.

Now, I get to meet the monster holding me here. For the first time since my captivity began, I get to meet Stonehart.

Whatever he wants, I'll be ready. The collar may be tight around my neck, but I will not be a prisoner.

A prisoner has no choice. A prisoner has no purpose.

But a concubine, on the other hand? She always has a choice.

And today, I choose to fight.

—

Uncovering You #2: Submission continues the story begun in *Uncovering You #1: The Contract*. It contains scenes of intense emotional and physical abuse. Readers with sensitivity to such subjects are advised to proceed with caution.

The story of *Uncovering You* unfolds over multiple volumes of approximately 125 pages each. Each volume is a fully-contained book with a climax and conclusion.

Books in the *Uncovering You* series will be released every 20 days. Here is the anticipated schedule:

Currently Available:
Uncovering You #1: The Contract
Uncovering You #2: Submission

Future Releases:
Uncovering You #3 - May 10, 2014
Uncovering You #4 - May 30, 2014
Uncovering You #5 - June 20, 2014

<u>Chapter One</u>

(Present day. Two weeks into stay.)

I feel his presence before he speaks.

"Well, well. Look at you."

Stonehart's voice is unmistakable. Raspy like the rustle of dry leaves, yet as strong as the most powerful gale on Olympus.

My back stiffens as I hear the *clap-clap* of loafers advancing on the marble floor.

"Presentable," he muses. I keep my eyes fixed on the column straight ahead. "Cleaned up. Though…" A pause. It takes all of my willpower not to turn my head. "…Disappointingly haggard," he concludes.

My hands curl into angry fists. That's a low blow.

I haven't seen myself in the mirror for weeks. But I can imagine how I must look. My entire body feels frail, stripped of the feminine curves it once possessed. I can see the sinewy muscles of my forearms move when I turn my wrist. I can feel the impression of my ribs when I slide my hand beneath my breasts. I am a walking skeleton, deprived of food, warmth, and human contact like some forgotten doll in the attic. All because of him.

And the bastard has the gall to call me *haggard*?

I turn in a rage, prepared to unleash a thousand obscenities that have been building in my mind the entire time I've been kept prisoner—and stop short when I find *him* a hair's breadth away.

Jeremy Stonehart is exactly the man I remember.

His melanite eyes regard me with a piercing intensity. Finely-trimmed stubble covering his cheeks gives prominence to his striking jaw and angular cheekbones. His wavy hair is loosely styled to casual perfection. Not a single strand is out of place.

His two-piece, silk Armani suit is tailored to his body like a second skin. The waist is trim, the shoulders wide and *high*. I'd forgotten how tall he is. The last time I saw him, I was wearing heels. Now, with him in his shoes and me barefoot, Stonehart towers above me like a malicious mountain.

"Chin up, now," he whispers. His finger trails a line up my neck. "Shoulders back. Atta girl. You want to look strong, yes?"

He sneers. "I know all about appearances, *Lilly*." The way he emphasizes my name makes me feel dirty, somehow. "And I know how little good they will do you."

He breaks away. I almost fall forward, whether from impulse or instinct, I don't know. Then, I remember the collar around my neck.

I look down at the floor and realize I'm right at the edge of my boundary. I stagger back, desperate to avoid the electric shock. My heart pounds like a drum.

Stonehart notices. He looks at me, then down at the floor, and then... smiles.

"Lilly," he says. "You needn't fear. The moment you signed the contract, you were afforded certain privileges." He takes out his phone and glances at the ceiling. "Look."

One swipe of his finger turns off all the lights. I can still see him, outlined by the light of his screen. He taps the phone, and a strange, deep purple light I've never seen here before fills the room.

Stonehart slips the phone back into his pocket. The ultra-violet light makes the white of his teeth and eyes the only thing visible when he speaks. It makes him look like an unearthly apparition.

"Look at the floor, Lilly. Do you see anything unusual?"

I swallow before answering. "No."

"You don't?" He sounds confused. Then he hits the side of his head as if just remembering. "Ah! Of course."

A malicious smile reveals those shining white teeth as Stonehart turns his phone back on. He does something I cannot see, and suddenly a thin red circle rushes in toward me along the floor. It stops right at the edge of my boundary.

"Do you know what that is, Lilly?"

His tone makes the blood drain from my face. I do not. But, it's not hard to guess. I shake my head, refusing to answer.

"Come now," Stonehart probes. "I'm sure you do. Take a gander."

I shake my head harder, making my hair swing in my eyes. I back away until my shoulder blades touch the marble beam. It might just be my imagination, but the red circle seems to be pulsing, constricting, and expanding ever-so-slightly under my watch.

My fingers clutch the collar. I pull at it in desperation, but to no effect.

Stonehart clicks his tongue. The purple light disappears, and with it the laser circle. All the overhead lights come back on.

"Lilly," he says. "Come here."

My eyes widen in terror as I look at him. He's outside my

boundary!

"No," I breathe."

"*Lilly!*" His voice snaps. "I told you once before how I hate repeating myself." He tilts his eyes ever so slightly. "Or have you forgotten?"

Damn it! I thought these power games would end when I signed the contract! "No," I muster. "But I can't. You're too far."

A vicious smile curls his handsome lips. "Are you refusing to obey?"

I shake my head. The collar feels like it's a live noose. "I can't—you're too far away!"

"Am I?" Stonehart seems amused. He holds both hands up as his eyes trail a path from his feet to mine. "It doesn't *seem* like I'm very far, does it? There's no physical barrier blocking your way."

Bile rises in my throat on hearing those god damn words spoken aloud. *No physical barrier.*

He takes one calculated step toward me. "There," he says. "I do not often compromise. But for you, I will. You say I'm too far. So I bridge the gap." His cruel eyes shine. "Now it's your turn."

I can hardly believe what I'm doing when I take my first

step toward him. My body shakes with apprehension. A cold sweat slicks my back. Stonehart is standing outside the perimeter. Reaching him would mean willingly subjecting myself to a second, horrible, electric shock.

But if I ever want to get back at him for everything that he has—and will—do to me, I have to submit to his games.

My senses are heightened in anticipation of the first tell-tale sign that I've gone too far as I walk forward. I stop on the edge of the boundary.

I am still fifteen feet away from Stonehart.

"To me, Lilly," he says softly, mockingly. "I want you by my side."

I grit my teeth and force myself to meet his evil stare. "I cannot."

"No?" His eyes glimmer. "Tell me why."

"*YOU KNOW WHY, YOU BASTARD!*" I scream.

My hands fly to my mouth when I realize what I've done. "I'm sorry," I whisper. "I—"

I am cut off by a sudden, booming laugh.

"So, you have some spark left in you, after all," he laughs. "Excellent. I knew your façade of weakness was just that. You, my dear, are not broken yet. Are you?"

Five quick strides and he's on me. His hand juts out and

grips my jaw, squeezing hard. My lips pucker together. He jerks my head up so my eyes meet his.

"But you will be," he promises, his voice soft and full of danger. "You will be tamed and trained to my liking."

He spins off and lets me go. The momentum drops me to my knees. I cry out when they strike the unforgiving floor.

Stonehart is back in his previous position, both hands clasped behind his back. His face is impassive, giving no hint of what has just occurred.

What kind of man can control his emotions so well?

"Now, Lilly," he commands. "To my side."

I stand up on unsteady legs. I glare at Stonehart with all the hate I can summon. He watches me, eyes shining, the corner of his mouth curled up in the barest hint of a smile.

I take one shaky step forward and flinch, waiting for the first warning shock.

I crack an eye open when it doesn't come. Stonehart tilts his head in acknowledgment. "Closer."

I close my eyes and try not to think about the black piece of plastic that's tight around my neck. Then, in a bout of either stupidity, lunacy, or desperation, I burst forward in a rush, feet slapping along the floor.

A solid grip on my arm stops me mid-run. I open my

eyes and see Stonehart smiling down at me. "That will be far enough. You wouldn't want to suffer another accident."

I look around, wide-eyed. "You extended the range," I breathe. I force down the gratitude that seems to spring from nowhere.

"I told you that your signature granted you privileges," Stonehart notes. "I am disappointed by your lack of faith in my word."

"I thought—"

"Remember, Lilly," he cuts me off, "that freedoms granted can just as easily be taken away."

He withdraws his phone, taps the screen a few times, and the purple UV light comes on. The thin red circle becomes visible, less than three inches away. I stare at it in horror, knowing how close I came to overstepping it.

"This is your boundary line," Stonehart observes. "Let me demonstrate the meaning of my words."

He taps a button on his phone. Immediately, the circle starts to shrink. I stare in bewilderment, too dumb to move.

"*Run,*" he whispers.

I spin back and sprint to my column. The laser circle nips at my heels. My heart is thundering and I'm gasping for air when my hands find the cool white stone. Stonehart's laughter echoes through the room.

I turn back, and am horrified to find the circle constricting past its initial boundary. Now it's only ten feet away. Five. *Three*.

It stops a bare inch away from my toes. I press myself against the marble as tight as I can. I don't dare move. I don't dare trigger the collar.

Stonehart's laughter continues. "You see?" he booms. "I am *always* in control. Do not forget that, Lilly."

As quickly as it had surrounded me, the red circle skitters away. I don't even see it on the ground anymore. The UV light turns off, and the bright ones come on.

I slump to the floor. My new clothes are ruined, drenched with sweat. I hang my head between my legs as I struggle through the constant, piercing pain that comes when my surroundings go from dark to light.

I hear Stonehart's footsteps on the floor as he walks a circle around me. "Now," he begins, "we have to go over the ground rules governing your behavior."

I manage to open my eyes long enough to see the triumphant expression on his face, just before he disappears from my field of vision. I refuse to turn my head to follow him.

One day, I will make him pay for this, I promise myself.

"Rule One." Stonehart's voice is sharp and clipped. "If you resist, or don't comply with a clause set out in the contract, you will suffer the *consequence of misbehavior.*" His intonation makes the labeling sound extremely ominous.

"Rule Two. You are explicitly prohibited from any form of self-harm. I will not have you—" he sneers at me, "— *spoiling* yourself."

"Three. You are not allowed to question my desires. Questions pertaining to your situation are prohibited." He kneels in front of me and I catch a whiff of his cologne. To think that it once functioned as an aphrodisiac is insane. "Do you understand, *Lilly*?"

I bite my tongue and nod, avoiding his eyes.

Stonehart stands up. "Good. You will not find me unreasonable, so long as you behave. Any requests you have will be given due consideration. But—" He pauses. "Do not test me."

I whimper and nod, even though it burns my pride to do so. He wants to see me broken, so I will *act* broken. It's the only chance I have of gaining any sort of advantage.

He *has* to underestimate me. But that will take time.

"Rule Four," Stonehart continues, pacing the room with

his hands behind his back. "I am a busy man. I will not always have time for you. However, you have no responsibilities other than pleasing me. I expect you to *always* be ready for me."

He stops and looks into my eyes. "Do you understand? The time I make for you is a privilege. Treat it as such. Dress and act accordingly."

"I understand," I answer. *Dress* accordingly? It's not like I own a wardrobe!

"Good. I will leave you those rules. Think on them. Your cooperation will result in increasingly greater freedoms. We will discuss their progression next time we meet." He walks over to the fully-curtained wall, and runs one hand up and down the rich fabric. "For now, it should be enough for you to know that the range of your collar has been extended to encompass all the rooms connected to this one. You can go through any unlocked doors you find."

"Doors?" I ask, slowly picking myself up. "What doors?"

Stonehart gestures behind him without glancing at me. "Some of the paintings you see hide entrances to this room. You will find a bathroom. A powder room. A closet. Feel free to make full use of the facilities at your disposal." He chuckles. "They are not there for me."

My heart lifts at the idea of a bathroom. A *proper* bathroom. There might even be a shower!

That means no more chamber pots. No more sponge baths—not that I have experienced more than one. Still, I was dreading the thought of the old woman coming back and cleaning me again. It was humiliating.

"I employ a full-time chef on my estate," Stonehart continues. "He is available to you. Through one door, you will find a small sitting room. There is a desk and paper. You may write down dietary requests and slip them under the locked door. Your meals will be rationed to prevent excessive weight gain, as is always a risk after a period of starvation. That does not mean your selection of food will be limited. You can have anything you want." He turns to me and smiles. "You see? I am not incapable of compassion."

"Thank you, Mr. Stone—"

"Jeremy," he corrects. "You will call me Jeremy."

I force a smile and give a slight curtsy. It's as close to being mocking as I dare. "Thank you, *Jeremy*."

"You're welcome, *Lilly*." Stonehart's dark eyes glisten when he says my name. "Tell me. Have you ever wondered what's behind this long curtain?"

"Every day," I answer.

A smile forms on his lips. "I will show you."

Stonehart takes a step back and retrieves his phone. He plays with the screen for half a second, Then, I hear a mechanical whirr.

My hands dart to my neck out of instinct.

Stonehart notices, and shakes his head. "No, Lilly. Not that. *This.*"

Suddenly, the great curtain begins to lift. It rises all along the massive expanse of the wall. Behind it is a thick, rubber-coated blackout drape, like an enormous projection screen. That one stays still until the curtain reaches the ceiling.

Then, it starts to follow. It lifts slowly. As soon as I see sunshine falling on the floor, I have an irrational urge to cry.

Behind the drape is a massive wall of glass. As the blackout drape lifts, sunlight floods the room. When the warmth reaches my skin, tears form in the corners of my eyes. I rub at them, angry and grateful at the same time.

The drape reaches the very top, and the floor-to-ceiling windows shimmer in the light. Beyond them is a stunning view of a magnificent vista, ending in a cliff ledge that gives way to the ocean.

Stonehart brings his wrist to a small sensor beside the single door in the glass wall. Just like in the elevator so long ago, I hear a *beep*, and the door unlocks. Stonehart opens it to leave, then stops halfway across the threshold and looks back at me.

"Lilly," he says, his voice stern and serious. "I will give you one week to return to the condition you were in when you entered my home. Eat, sleep, and rest. You have no obligation to me for the next seven days. Right now, you are skinny, wretched, and unattractive. When I see you next, I expect to be greeted by the vibrant, young woman you once were."

With that, he walks out into the light.

Chapter Two

I wait a long time before gathering my courage and testing my new boundary. I expect to feel the warning shock with every step I take past my former perimeter.

With that type of caution, it takes a good five minutes to creep to the glass wall.

My fingers tremble as I lay them against the cool glass. The sun is so bright. So warm.

I breathe onto the glass to fog it, then wipe the condensation with the side of my hand, just to make sure it's real.

Everything feels so surreal right now. I look past the glass and try to wrap my mind around all that's been hidden from me these last few tortuous weeks. My room—this room— sits on a massive estate built into the side of a cliff. The view is magnificent. Beautiful, red rock extends a hundred yards from where I stand, and then gives way to a jagged ledge that forms a sheer drop into the ocean.

The ocean. The *Pacific* Ocean, beautiful and unmarred. If I take a deep breath, I can almost smell the tangy, salty, sea mist—even through the glass. The water is still today. The red rays reflecting off it make it seem like a pool of rubies.

I turn around. The sunlight filling the room makes it seem so much more hospitable. It's almost enough to make it seem more like a palace than a dungeon.

A palace with no way out, I remind myself.

Admittedly, I feel a little thrill getting to explore. Stonehart said the paintings cover doors. I want to see that for myself.

I walk around the outside of the massive room, completing one full circle while trailing a hand along the walls. After spending so many hours confined to the pillar, I have no desire to return to that dreadful spot.

I walk up to each of the paintings, examining them, one by one. I see the hinges on some of them, along with an opposing latch. I mark those in my mind but do not open them.

Not yet. I want to enjoy every second of sunlight that I can.

I stop in front of the glass door that Stonehart used to leave. He said I could go through any unlocked door, did he not? And I won't know what type *this* one is until I try.

I'm not expecting miracles here.

My hand clasps the handle. I push down. It doesn't

budge.

I smother my disappointment. I knew in the back of my mind that this door would be locked. Only desperation led me to expect otherwise.

I may be a lot of things. I may *act* a lot of things, for Stonehart's sake… but *desperate* is something I can never allow myself to become.

Because I need to be clear-minded and lucid if I am to plan my revenge.

My stomach growls, reminding me of food. I sigh. Even after the feast the old woman brought me, my body is crying out for nutrition. My next meal doesn't arrive until tomorrow morning. She told me so.

That means I have all night to explore.

Chapter Three

Behind the first painting is a short hallway with two doors at the end. I walk slowly, always mindful of triggering my collar. Stonehart may have said I could wander without worry, but can I really trust him to tell the truth?

The door to my right opens to a majestic bathroom. Shining tiles line the floor. All the appliances are gilded gold. My eyes take in the titular bathtub. It is already filled with water. I dip my hand in, and am delighted to find it warm.

Soaking in a tub is a privilege I have not had in years. I close the door for privacy—then stumble when I can't find any way to lock it.

Of course you can't lock it, you dolt. Stonehart wouldn't let you bar yourself away.

A shiver crawls up my spine as I remember his words: "The time I make for you is a privilege."

Suddenly, all desire for a hot bath vanishes. I am to be a sex slave. A *pampered* sex slave, perhaps, but a sex slave nonetheless.

I am halfway out of the room before I change my mind again. Stonehart said he would leave me alone for a week.

That promise gives me a sense of security, false as it may be. I should not worry about him yet.

You have five years for that, a small voice reminds me.

I shake my head. *No.* No! I have no intention of letting things last that long.

Mustering all my dignity, I disrobe and slip into the water, chin held high. I even pull the door open behind me.

I won't have Stonehart think I am frightened.

My muscles quickly relax in the luxurious water. There's a cupboard filled with assorted salts, soaps, and shampoos nearby. The only thing missing is a mirror.

An hour or two later—I lost track of time in the tub—I step out of the bathroom with a lush, thick towel wrapped under my armpits. I could almost imagine I'm alone in a magnificent hotel suite… were it not for the collar around my neck.

I hate that collar. I hate what it represents. I hate what it can do. It will never let me forget that I am a prisoner.

But, because of that, I will never forget my need for revenge.

The door across the hall is closed but not locked. I pry it open slowly—and am greeted by the most amazing powder room I've ever laid eyes on.

A waist-high, granite counter top is stocked with enough beauty tools to make a makeup artist blush. Rows of lipstick in every shade fill one shelf. Eyeliner, eye shadow, moisturizers, powders, and all sorts of accessories fill another. All are from the most expensive beauty brands.

If Fey ever saw this room, she would die of pure joy.

Of course, there is also a mirror. I see my reflection for the first time in weeks. I barely recognize the girl staring back at me.

Stonehart was right: I look awful.

My skin is pale from lack of sun. My eyes have dark bags under them. My cheeks are hollow and sagging from poor nutrition. My lips, which have always been so naturally red that I never had the need for lipstick, are now a pallid gray. The usual shine in my eyes is gone, replaced by an empty lifelessness.

Anger flares inside of me. All of it is directed at *him. He* made me like this. *He* is the reason I am unrecognizable. I turn sideways to take in my profile. I'm so skinny I'm afraid the smallest gust of wind will blow me away.

Stonehart starved me, deprived me of everything, and then he has the goddamn nerve to call me *wretched?*

Calm down, Lilly, the voice of reason whispers in my head.

Do __not__ react to his words. They are meant to incite you!

I relax my hands so my nails don't draw blood from my palms. The voice is right. I gain nothing by responding to him this way.

I need to keep my emotions in check. But I will forget nothing he does. I will have vengeance, and I *will* bring Stonehart down.

I walk out of the powder room without touching so much as a speck. I have no desire for makeup.

Besides, I want to have ammunition in case Stonehart reneges on his word. He said I have seven days to myself. If he breaks his promise, and comes earlier, he will not find a woman looking her best.

I walk back to the room with the pillar. I decided to call it the sunroom while I was in the tub. Better than calling it a prison.

I make an annoyed sound in my throat after thinking of the term 'prison.' I promised myself that I would not refer to any part of this estate by that name.

It's not that I'm trying to delude myself. Not at all. I want to avoid using that term to steel myself in my purpose.

A *prisoner* has no purpose. A *prisoner* has no choice.

But a *concubine*, on the other hand? She always has a

choice.

Besides, truly: what better way is there to destroy something—or in this case, some*one*—than from the inside out?

Stonehart has his own reasons for keeping me here. I suspect they go deeper than his baser desires. But I have my own reasons for staying, too.

Fool! It's not like you can just walk out!

I shake my head to silence that voice. The only way to keep my sanity—the only way to have some semblance of control—is to make myself believe that I am here for my own reasons. If I truly want to take down Stonehart Industries—and the man with it—I need to be smart. I need to bide my time. I need to ingratiate myself to him, to appear weak, and harmless, and above all, *nothing* like a threat. I need him to *think* he is winning.

Because the moment he lets down his guard… this mouse will transform into a viper.

Pleased with my plan of attack, I walk about the sunroom and investigate the areas beyond the other paintings.

I find the sitting room next. It has a small desk and a stool, along with one locked door that I assume is monitored from the other side. I write down my request for breakfast on a piece of paper and slip it underneath, just like Stonehart told me to do.

I walk back out and go up to the final painting. It's clever, I think, how the architect was able to disguise the doorways with these pieces of art. Judging by what I've seen of the structure, this estate was built recently.

I unclasp the latch and pull it open, not knowing what to expect inside…

My eyes go wide and I forget to breathe. Behind painting number three is the biggest room of all. In fact, it might rival the size of my entire Palo Alto apartment.

I walk in and stare in disbelief. This room is a *closet*. It's a fully-stocked, giant *closet*. There are as many clothes here as you would expect to find in the back of a Nordstrom's or Saks'.

One wall is lined with shoes. There are pumps and sandals, heels and boots. There are oxfords and wedges and platforms, some in rich leathers, others lined with fur.

I pick up a pair at random and slip them onto my feet. They are a perfect fit.

I see a rack of robes tucked away in a corner. I drop my towel in haste and run across, then wrap myself in the first one that I reach. I hug the luxurious fabric to my skin and breathe deep, loving the scent of clean, new fabric.

Feeling, for the first time in a long time, comfortable and cozy, I stroll amongst the remaining racks. I run my hands through the hanging garments. Blouses, jackets, skirts, dresses, stockings, scarves, and a million other pieces of clothing all fill the room.

All of them are for me.

Suddenly, I feel nauseous. The closet has only one entrance that I can see. It's only accessible from the sunroom.

That means all these clothes were here for me *before* I arrived.

Holy shit! How long had Stonehart been planning my abduction?

A cold sweat grips me as I sit down hard. Stonehart's assistant said she'd been looking for me when she called. I assumed she meant that day, but what if the search had been going on for weeks? Months?

The clothes confirm I am not some random victim. No, I am stuck in the middle of some unknown web of Stonehart's making.

But why me? I wrack my brain but find no answer. What interest can a man of Stonehart's stature possibly have in *me*?

I have no family other than my mother, and I haven't

spoken to her in years. I have no sisters or brothers, no cousins, or distant relatives. I don't even have a boyfriend! I should be completely anonymous as far as Stonehart is concerned.

But, I'm not. Why? How? When did he first take an interest in me?

I have no idea. But I swear on everything I'm worth that I *will* find out.

I get back up. The clothes pose a riddle I have no answer for. But if there's one thing I possess in abundance, it's time. Time enough to figure this out.

One other thought strikes me as I leave the room: *I don't see any lingerie anywhere.*

Chalk up one more personality quirk to my captor.

Chapter Four

I wake up the next morning to the rising sun. Feeling the warm rays on my face after two long weeks in the dark is surreal. A jumble of emotions bubbles up inside: joy, disbelief, excitement.

A few minutes later, I get up and walk into the sitting room, following the smell of food. I find a generous portion of all that I've asked for waiting for me on the desk. I carry the plates back to the sunroom, sit down close to the glass, and have breakfast looking out at the magnificent ocean before me.

I have nothing to do when I finish, so I bring out a towel from the bathroom and lie on it on the floor in the sun. The late September rays aren't as strong as they would have been just a few weeks ago. But I want to soak up as much vitamin D as I can. Doing that always improves my mood.

As I lie there, I reflect on how much things have changed since I signed the contract. I may be only two days removed from my previous, near-death condition, but, already, I feel like a woman transformed.

It's funny how much a bit of perceived freedom can lift a

person up.

Yet, that's exactly what this newfound freedom is: *Perceived.* I am not really free. I am completely at Stonehart's mercy.

He's given me seven days to recuperate. What happens after, when the contract *really* kicks in?

I close my eyes and take a steadying breath. Whatever happens, I will face it holding onto my true purpose with an iron grip.

I *will* be ready for him when he comes. And one day, he will learn that he chose the wrong girl as his plaything.

A bell chimes behind me, startling me to my knees. I whip back and look around, but find the room empty.

It sounds once more, from down the hall leading to the sitting room.

Curious but cautious, I start slowly toward the room. I've never heard that bell before, and new things in my surroundings must be approached with due respect.

Halfway there, the smell of freshly-cut strawberries hits my nose. I rush forward, and discover lunch waiting for me.

There's a huge bowl of berries, accompanied by a tall glass of water. The succulent smell of the fruits is almost enough to make me weepy again. After being deprived of food for so long, each meal is a blessing.

I'm in the process of stuffing a handful in my mouth when I notice an envelope tucked under the glass. I put the berries down, feeling an ominous threat growing in the back of my mind. Carefully, I wipe my hands on a cloth and pick the envelope up.

There are two pieces of paper inside. Both are folded, but I can see through the back. One has handwriting on it. The other has printed text.

I unfold the handwritten one first.

I hope you are enjoying your food today. I want to remind you that freedom comes with a price.

Do not neglect the body shape clause in our contract. Nothing angers me more than sloppiness.

- J.S.

PS: Attached you will find my test results from yesterday morning. I hope they ease your lingering concerns.

PPS: You should know that a pregnancy is unacceptable. I took the liberty of slipping your first birth control pill into your breakfast this morning. The others will be given to you whole. I expect full compliance in this matter.

I stare at the note in disbelief. The bastard drugged me—
again! It's not so much the drug that bothers me. It's the *act*
of doing it. What else has he been sneaking into my meals?

I crumple the note and hurl it against the opposite wall.
My appetite for the berries is gone. In fact, in one angry
move, I sweep everything off the table—berries, bowl, and
all. The plate and glass hit the floor and shatter.

I leap up off the stool and stomp out of the room. I'm so
angry I could scream. I feel like I'm suffocating!

No amount of rationalization can change the truth. I *am* a
prisoner, and I *am* entirely at Stonehart's mercy. He can do
with me whatever the hell he wants, and I have absolutely no
say in the matter!

I pace back and forth through the sunroom, my strides
sharp and livid. The ocean outside mocks me. The sunlight
reflecting off the glass mocks me. I can see all of it, but it
might as well be an image on a television screen for all the
good it brings me.

I need to break free. Right *now*, I need to break free!

I stride to the closest painting. This one does not hide a
door. I steady myself beneath it, hook my fingers under the
edge, and heave. It comes off its hooks. It's heavy and

awkward, and I nearly lose my balance as it lifts off.

But, I catch myself in time. I stagger over with it toward the giant glass wall. Then, with one great heave, I throw the painting against the glass with as much strength as I have.

I don't know why I expected the glass to break. Obviously, it's stronger than that. The painting bounces off and clatters to the floor.

I grip my hair in my hands and scream in frustration. My voice echoes through the hollow room.

Of *course* the glass won't break. Of *course* there's no way out. And even if I did manage to break a panel, what good would it do? I still have the fucking collar around my neck!

Having nowhere else to go, I stalk up to my pillar, cross my arms, and lean against it, brooding.

***

Eventually, common sense gets the better of me.

I was acting like a child. Trying to break free? A waste of effort. Stonehart obviously took precautions to ensure that escape is impossible. At least, escape in the expected way.

My tantrum came from a place of desperation and hopelessness. I promised myself that I would not succumb to those feelings. Doing so is as good as admitting defeat.

And Lilly Ryder is far from defeated.

I pick myself up and walk back to the sitting room. There, I squat down and clean the remains of my lunch from the floor. I find the crumpled ball of paper and straighten it against my leg. Stonehart *wants* his actions to affect me. When I react the way I did, I play right into his hands.

I will not give him the satisfaction of getting an explosive reaction from me again.

I place the note back into the envelope. Then, as curiosity gets the better of me, I unfold the second sheet.

It shows the result of an STD test. All came back negative. But that's not what interests me most.

The date is.

The note said Stonehart took the test yesterday. The date on the sheet reads *November 10th, 2013*.

November 10th. That means today is the 11th.

I fight off the wave of dizziness that tries to take me. I haven't been here for two weeks.

I've been here for *five*.

How had I miscounted so badly? The days all blurred together in the dark. But if *today* is the eleventh, that means I held out for... for a month and a half.

I don't know whether to feel angry or proud. Angry at myself for my stubbornness. Proud of remaining steadfast in my initial purpose.

In the end, I settle for a mixture of the two. Knowing that it's been over a month makes so much sense. It makes my stunning weight loss less remarkable. But what kind of blasted ideal of stubbornness, of stupidity, had me fight my war of attrition for *five weeks*?

The bit of pride I feel for holding out is probably misplaced, but so be it. I can't help that.

There are other pieces of information of interest to me in the paper. The most shocking is Stonehart's birthday: June 10th, 1970. The man is forty-three, yet he could pass for a thirty-year-old!

I put that paper back into the envelope. I hate the mocking way he wrote that the test results should "ease my concerns."

And yet, a part of me—albeit, a very, very small part— does appreciate the gesture. I guess it might be seen as chivalric, in a twisted, totally sadistic kind of way.

I sit there, alone with my thoughts, when a realization strikes me.

Nothing I do matters until Stonehart makes his presence known.

I need to learn about who he is as a man in order to exploit his weakness. But, I cannot do that without him around.

The real games begin in six days. Until then, I must do everything in my power to get ready.

Chapter Five

One day goes by, followed by the next, and the next again. The food I am given makes my body feel stronger. The sun I soak in fills me with resolve. I have nothing to do, yet the freedom to simply roam with no fear of triggering my collar is enough to keep me from boredom.

I have no idea what Stonehart will do to me when he returns—well, I have some idea, but it doesn't mean I enjoy thinking about it. No matter what, I will not wait in apprehension.

I will be ready for him when he comes back. He will find me perfectly willing and perfectly submissive.

Of course, that will just be an act that drives me to my true purpose.

Besides, I know how little good resistance will do. Moreover, I know the expectations that come from the contract. I agreed to play his game. I cannot back down now.

Five days into my wait, I catch my reflection in the enormous glass wall at night. I can't help but smile. I've already put on weight, and my cheeks are starting to get their regular glow back. Having access to a bathroom, limitless clothing, food, and sunlight definitely helps. Fresh air would be a nice addition, but I'm in no state to complain.

The night before Stonehart's expected arrival, I take extra pains to make myself presentable. I soak in the perfumed waters of the tub for hours, making my skin soft and pink. I wash my hair and style it in the most elegant fashion I know. I've already picked out what I'm going to wear, and laid it out on the floor for after my bath.

I apply some blush to my cheeks, eye shadow to my eyelids, and a tiny bit of lip gloss. Nobody who saw me a week ago would ever guess I am the same person today.

I remember the big deal Stonehart made about precision the night I met him in the restaurant. He told me seven days when he left, and seven days is what he will hold me to.

I fully expect him to arrive at midnight.

The last time I saw him, he left by way of the door. I sit facing it with my back against the marble pillar, and begin my wait.

***

It's been hours since nightfall. My eyes are drooping shut. My head keeps falling forward. Each time it does, I jerk back up, refusing to give in to sleep.

The anticipation is killing me. When will Stonehart come? What will he want? How will he react when he sees me?

Those thoughts threaten to take me down a slippery slope. I shiver and rub my arms, not wanting to let my imagination give way to fear.

**

I wake up with a jolt. The early rays of the sun fill the room.

Immediately, my eyes focus on the other person present. Stonehart is standing at one of the glass panes, facing away from me. He looks absolutely striking in a crisp beige suit. He's holding a clear goblet of wine behind his back.

My mind races and panic sets in. How long has he been there? Oh God, how long has he been *waiting*?

Stonehart glances over his shoulder a split-second after I wake. "Oh. Did I startle you? By all means, take your time."

I scramble up, straightening my clothes in the process. "Jeremy," I say, flustered. "You should have woken me."

"I couldn't do that," he mocks. "You looked so beautiful asleep."

I have no idea whether to take the comment as a compliment or jeer.

"Don't worry," he continues, turning toward me. As he walks closer, I notice the fine lines around his eyes. Though the suit looks freshly pressed, the shirt underneath is wrinkled. His tie is loose. I wonder absently if he's been working all night.

"I am not angry with you," Stonehart tells me. "In fact, I have something for you. A gift." He stops in front of me. "Lilly. Hold out your hand."

I remember what he said about the *consequences of misbehavior*. I don't know what those are, but I am not keen on finding out. I lift up my right arm and extend it to him.

He cups my hand gently between both of his. His grip is firm yet tender. A small gasp escapes my mouth at the warmth I feel around my fingers.

I've thought of him as this horrible monster for so long that it's a shock to realize that warm blood runs through his veins, like mine.

He smiles at my reaction, then strokes my fingers with his thumb. That small gesture is so endearing that it frightens me. It feels like the caress of a lover, not a captor.

Stonehart slowly brings my hand to his lips and kisses it.

The hairs on my arms stand up. I suppress a shiver.

Dammit, how can my body react to him this way?

"I am pleased," he says softly, his deep, angelic voice lifting my soul, "with the way you have improved your appearance since my last visit. So, I brought you this."

One of his hands reaches into his pocket, and he pulls out a small velvet box. I see the word *Buccellati* emblazoned upon it in fine, silver lettering.

"For you," he says.

"What is it?"

"Open it, and see."

I accept the little box. My fingers tremble as they run over the sides. I open it, and stare.

Inside is a beautiful diamond ring. It catches the light and scatters it into millions of different rays. I've never seen anything like it.

"Why?" is all I manage.

"As a token of my appreciation," Stonehart replies. I reach out hesitatingly with my thumb and stroke the diamond. I don't quite believe it's real. "You might think of it as… a *token of good behavior*. Here. Let me."

He takes the box from my hand and picks up the ring. I hold my hand suspended in the air as he slides it over my ring finger. It fits above my knuckle like a dream.

"Do you like it?" he asks.

"Yes," I whisper. "I like it very much."

"Good." Stonehart smiles. "I am pleased."

At that moment, I catch a dangerous glimmer in his eye. It makes me take an involuntary step back.

"*Lilly.*" Stonehart emphasizes my name as his eyes pierce into me. "Every good deed deserves a reward."

My heart starts racing as I realize what he means. I've been preparing myself for this, but actually going through with it… it's a different story. The look on his face tells me exactly what he wants.

His hands jut out and clasp my shoulders. He presses down, forcing me to my knees. "Consider this," he says, unzipping his pants, "…a small taste of things to come."

His hand twists hard into my hair and he jerks me to him. "Be a good girl, now, and don't bite."

***

I splash my face with cold water again and again, trying to erase the memory of what just happened.

The minute Jeremy's pants came off, he became… an

45

animal. I could feel him channeling all his suppressed rage into me. He didn't care if I choked, didn't care if he pulled my hair so hard it was almost ripped from its roots. All he cared about was getting his pleasure, *showering me with his release*, and then… turning around and leaving.

I cringe as I try to wipe a string of semen from my hair. Having it touch my skin fills me with disgust. I toss the soiled paper napkin into the toilet and press the flush lever with my toe.

Feeling slightly cleaner, but no less used, I drag myself to the powder room to take in my reflection.

There are a few popped blood vessels in my forehead from when he wrapped his hands around my neck and cut off circulation. I can cover those up with a modest brushing. My eyes are rimmed red from the tears that ran down my face. I check the drawers for some Visine, find it, and put a few drops in each eye. Stonehart said to expect him again today, and of course, that means keeping up appearances.

I set to it.

***

I prop myself up against the countertop when I'm done.

46

It's amazing how much a little makeup can transform a person's appearance.

I look as radiant as ever.

I hold my shoulders high and waltz out to select my evening attire. When Stonehart left me, I was a huddling mess on the floor. When he sees me next, he will find no sign of that woman.

Determination to see justice done keeps my spirit from breaking. Stonehart wants to prove to me that he owns my body. I will let him indulge in that fantasy.

This is only day one.

Chapter Six

I come back to the sunroom to an unexpected surprise. The door leading outside is open.

For a moment, my brain cannot comprehend what this means. Am I allowed out? Is this another so-called "token of good behavior"?

Only after grappling with those thoughts do I notice a dining table being set up by the same elderly woman who cared for me that day a week ago. She stops what she's doing when she notices me, and smiles.

"You are looking the picture of health this morning, Miss Ryder."

I blink, surprised to be addressed by anyone other than Stonehart. I am so used to being forgotten. Old habits die hard, I guess.

"Oh," I stammer. "Thank you." I take a few careful steps toward her. "I'm sorry, but I never caught your name."

"It's Rose." She smiles again, then turns her attention back to the table.

"Rose," I mumble under my breath. It's amazing to be talking to someone *other* than Stonehart. "It's nice to meet you, Rose."

She makes a noncommittal but friendly gesture toward me without glancing up.

I walk a few more steps toward her. "I was wondering, since you left the door open…" I eye the tray of dishware standing outside, "…if that means that…" I trail off, not sure how much to say.

"Oh!' She stands straight and puts her hands on her hips. "Actually, Mr. Stonehart did ask me to pass a message onto you. He said, 'Nothing has changed.' Now," she laughs, "I won't presume to know what that means, and it's certainly not my intention to pry, but I suspect you have some sort of agreement with him? Maybe this has something to do with that."

She winks at me, cheerful as a honeybee. "He also told me to make sure to always keep that door closed, but it was so stuffy in here when I came, I thought a little fresh air might do you good." She smiles. "Don't you agree?"

"Oh, yes," I whisper, astounded. Fresh air? Is it possible that I have found an ally in this woman?

I can hardly believe she is the person who regarded me with such disinterest a week ago.

"Do you mind?" I ask, gesturing to the door.

"By all means," she says. "Be my guest."

I walk up to the door and put my hands on the frame. A draft lifts my hair around my face. I inhale deeply, loving the scent of the ocean. I haven't tasted fresh air in God knows how long.

It feels like an enormous breach of protocol to be doing this. But I am not breaking any rules, am I? And knowing that I am feeling the wind on my face—something Stonehart had no intention of allowing me to do—is an encouraging boost to my psyche.

Stonehart does not control as much as he thinks.

I wonder how far I'm willing to push this time. I look down at my feet, then edge them forward a few inches. My toes hang over the threshold.

I know the collar tracks my position. As long as my head stays inside, I shouldn't be in any danger.

I take a deep breath and close my eyes, then stick one foot out the door.

A great thrill shoots through me when my foot touches the cement walkway outside. I shiver and pull back quickly. One taste of rebellion is enough.

I walk up to Rose. I see her hide a small smile as she keeps her eyes pointed downward.

"Are you setting up for me and Mr. St—Jeremy?" I ask.

"Yes," she answers.

"He didn't tell me he was coming for dinner."

"At six o'clock," Rose confirms.

"Hmm." I have hours left yet. With nothing else to do, I ask, "May I help you?"

Rose looks at me. A kind, motherly smile graces her lips. "I'd like that very much.

Chapter Seven

Some hours later, I'm sitting alone at the table, looking over the beautiful water, when I catch Stonehart approaching from the corner of my eye. I stand as he enters the room, and only sit back down when he takes his chair across from me.

"Good evening, Lilly," he greets me.

"Good evening, Jeremy," I reply.

"I see you were waiting for me. That's good." He takes a small sip of water. "I hate it when it's the other way around."

"I promise, that won't happen again." I offer a sickly-sweet smile.

"Good." Stonehart nods. He leans back and drapes one arm over his chair. "You look beautiful tonight, Lilly."

His voice is completely sincere. It takes me by surprise.

"Thank you, Jeremy."

"The color of your dress brings out your eyes," he observes. "I am pleased you took the effort to find suitable clothes."

"It's not hard when I have such a generous selection at my disposal."

Stonehart nods in approval. "I have to say, your behavior is a pleasant surprise. I was expecting more… defiance… from you."

I smile at him sweetly. "Why would you expect defiance, Jeremy? You provide me with everything that I need."

He smirks. "Yes. You might say that." He glances over his shoulder. "Shall we eat?"

On his word, a young man in a tuxedo bustles in from the sitting room. He wheels a tray of food with him. Delectable scents waft from the covered platter.

He sets up the table with practiced efficiency. Stonehart does not acknowledge him until he's done, and I take his cue. We both wait in silence.

When the young man is finished, Stonehart gives a curt nod of dismissal. The man bows, turns, and walks away.

When we're alone again, Stonehart smiles. "How was your day?" he asks.

I stare at him as my brain goes blank. I nearly forget myself enough to let my jaw drop. *How was my day?* Is he fucking *serious*?

"Lilly," he notes, "it's customary to reply to a polite inquiry at dinner."

"It was fine," I sputter, shaking my head. "How was

53

yours?"

Stonehart's eyes narrow. The movement is so slight it'd be imperceptible to most people. I pick up on it. I know better than to let my guard down around him. Not when so much depends on his moods.

"Need I remind you of the rules governing your behavior?" Stonehart asks, his eyes growing hard. "Rule three, in particular: You are not allowed to question my desires. Questions pertaining to your situation are prohibited," he quotes.

My stomach instantly twists into a knot. "No, Jeremy, I didn't mean it that way. I'm sorry. It just—slipped out." I lower my eyes to my plate. "Please don't punish me," I whisper.

"Now, now, Lilly." Stonehart speaks with rich, mocking warmth. "What need would I have to punish you? I'm not immune to your situation. I understand some of your social abilities have dulled over the course of your stay. That just adds one more item to the list of things we need to work on."

"I'll do better," I promise, silently cursing myself. Groveling goes against every bone in my body, but it's what I must do if I want to play my role right. "You're right. I'm rusty."

"Of course I'm right," he tells me. "You'd be hard-pressed to find a situation in which I'm wrong."

Except about me, I repeat in my head. *You're wrong about me.*

Stonehart smiles. I'd call it a greasy smile if it were on a face even a tenth less handsome. But he has clearly mastered the art of presentation. Everything about him flows from a place of cool confidence. "Shall we eat?"

"Yes," I agree, glad for a distraction. "Yes, let's."

***

The rest of dinner goes by without much in the way of conversation. I don't know my place yet, so I don't speak unless Stonehart asks me a direct question.

That attitude fosters a growing silence between us. It has me on edge. Stonehart, on the other hand, looks right at ease. As he eats, he directs a polite smile at me every once in a while. The quiet does not bother him.

Then again, why should it? I imagine he has dealt with situations that were orders of magnitude more stressful—and important—than a dinner with his... *plaything*. To him, this dinner means nothing.

But for me, interactions like this are of utmost importance. One-on-one time with Stonehart is the only chance I have to learn about him.

This is his mask, I realize just as I'm taking my last bite. *This is the face he shows to his colleagues. To the public. This is the face of Jeremy Stonehart, mega-millionaire, CEO of Stonehart Industries.*

It gives no hint of the monster lurking underneath.

After our plates are taken away, Stonehart leans back. He still hasn't said anything. He smiles, and I feel his eyes taking my features in. They dip past my neck, to the hemline of my dress. Being openly ogled like that makes me uncomfortable. I want to tug the straps up, and hide more of my skin, but I am sure that doing so would irritate him.

So, I sit perfectly straight and pretend not to notice.

Eventually, the silence becomes unbearable. This is the most time I've spent with him without having his cock shoved down my throat. I need to take advantage, especially so long as we're both operating on some pretense of civility.

"Jeremy?" I venture. I make sure to add the proper amount of hesitation to my voice. "May I ask you a question?"

He picks up his wineglass and swirls it in his hand. "Do you remember our rules?" he asks.

"Yes. My question—well, it's not even a question, really, more like… a clarification. It has to do with your—with my—rules. I'm only asking so I don't risk breaking them later."

Stonehart leans forward, intrigued. "You're taking initiative," he says. "You're owning your situation. I respect that." He nods. "Go on."

I clear my throat. "You mentioned, before… um, *consequences of misbehavior.*"

"Yes," he says. "I did."

"I was wondering…" I clear my throat again. "What those would be?"

Stonehart smiles grandly. "Why, Lilly. I didn't think a smart girl like you would have any trouble figuring that out." He pauses to lean back and crosses one leg over the other. "The answer's simple:

"If you misbehave, I will leave you in the dark."

All the blood drains from my brain. *No. No, I will not go back there!*

My grip on my own wineglass slackens. It slips through my fingers and falls to the floor, splintering into tiny, sharp shards. The red liquid spreads like a growing pool of blood.

Stonehart frowns. "I've upset you," he says softly. "Lilly,

I assure you, that was not my intention."

"It's my fault," I stammer, shaking my head. There is no act this time. This reaction is wholly my own. "I just… I just need…"

"Yes?" Stonehart asks, leaning forward. "Lilly. Tell me what you need."

"I need… I need… *air*!"

I gasp and push up from the table. I stumble as a wave of light-headedness hits me.

Stonehart is by my side in a flash. His hands gently grip my shoulders and he lowers me to my chair.

"Breathe," he tells me. "Lower your head." I see him looking up at me, and realize he's kneeling down to be on my level. I see both compassion *and* concern on his face.

Damn him for being such a good actor! Nobody in their right mind would ever think those emotions are faked. But I know better.

Stonehart holds my hand between both of his. I should be repulsed by having him so close, but somehow, beyond all reason, that simple grip on my hand gives me strength.

"Do you need some water?" he asks. Holy hell! He even manages to make his *voice* sound sincere. "You said you need air. Would you like to go outside?"

I nod dumbly. Stonehart stands, looping one arm around my waist, and helps me up. I have to lean on him for support as he leads me forward.

We walk to the door. I'm breathing quickly, taking sharp, little gasps as I force my feet to move. It feels like I'm close to a panic attack.

Stonehart stops in front of the glass door and brings his wrist to the sensor. I hear the beep of the scanner—and remember the still-active collar around my neck.

I push away from Stonehart and stare, wide-eyed, as cool, sweet night air rushes in from the gaping door.

"The range," I half-gasp. "Did you change it?"

Stonehart looks at me with pity. "My sweet Lilly," he says. "The moment I change the range, you will be the first to know."

My eyes dart to the door. My hands are balled into fists at my side. My heart is racing. "You were going to lead me outside," I say, trying to make sense of it. "*Past* the perimeter you set?"

Stonehart spreads his arms. I catch a filthy, malicious glimmer in his eye. "You said that's where you wanted to go."

White hot rage erupts in me like an inferno. "You

59

BASTARD!" I scream. "You knew what would happen if I stepped over the threshold!"

"Lilly, Lilly," he chastises. "There's no need to raise your voice. Of course I knew. As did you. But who am I to deny a lady's request?"

"You knew what would happen!" I accuse. "You knew, and you still led me there!" I must be mad, to be screaming at him like this.

Stonehart takes one strong step toward me. "You keep yelling at me, Lilly, and you risk making me angry." His smile deepens. "I don't think you'll like me when I'm angry."

"Like you? *I hate you!*" Insanity has definitely taken its hold. The buffer between my thoughts and my speech has disappeared. "You're sick! What kind of a man does that to a woman? To a stranger! Who am I to you, Jeremy? You're sick, twisted, and *I FUCKING HATE YOU!*"

Stonehart takes in my tirade with a calm and steady grace. I'm gasping for breath by the end. Every fiber of my body is trembling, strung tight.

"Are you quite done?" he asks in a soft, cool voice.

I answer by stalking to the table, picking up the bottle of wine, and flinging it at his face.

He ducks out of the way of the projectile. It smashes

against the glass panel behind him and shatters.

Stonehart growls, and advances on me. He moves fast. I jump back, but his hands dart out to catch me.

I struggle in his grip, trying to break free. "Let go!"

His fingers dig into my arms. It hurts. "Look at me," he commands.

I shake my head with reckless abandon. *What happened to calm, rational Lilly?* a voice in the far-reaches of my mind asks. *What happened to the girl who would bide her time?*

"Fine. Your choice." His hand jerks up and tangles in my hair. He closes his fist, ruthlessly pulling my roots.

Pain shoots from his grip, runs down my spine, and overtakes my body. It's enough to draw tears.

Stonehart forces my head up. I whimper like a frightened child. He's so much bigger than I am, so much stronger. He can manhandle me with absolutely no effort.

I'm terrified of what I'm going to find in his eyes. I squeeze mine shut harder, trying to escape from this nightmare.

His hand digs into my hair even more. "Open your eyes," he commands. "Open your eyes, and face me, Lilly."

Adrenaline is shooting through my body with every heartbeat. My breathing is ragged. The pain running from the back of my scalp is so bad it's unbearable. Still, I refuse to open my eyes.

"I will tell you once more," Stonehart says. "Or, are you refusing to comply?"

No. No! I will not be left in the dark again!

I crack one eye open, then the other, and face the monster I've enraged. The moment I see his burning glare, the darkness does not seem like such a bad alternative.

"I will answer your questions in the order you posed them," he tells me, his chopped diction the only indication of his emotions. "What kind of man am I? The kind who *can*, Lilly. And the kind who *does*. I *can* do this to you, so I *do*." His hand tightens in my hair, making me gasp. I blink rapidly against the swell of tears.

"Who are you to me? You're my *employee*, and, as an extension of that, my *property*. You remain so for the duration of our contract." He lowers his face to mine. I can feel his breath on my skin. "You haven't forgotten that, have you?" He twists my hair, making my cry out. "Well? Answer me!"

"N-no!" I cry.

"No. You say 'no,' Lilly. But, I think that you have forgotten. In fact, I think I've been too lenient with you." He pulls so hard that I'm sure my hair will rip free at any moment.

"Please," I beg. "Please, you're hurting me."

A sinister smirk forms on his lips. "You don't enjoy this?" he asks, his eyes moving from my face to his hand and back again. "You don't like being *handled* this way?"

Tears blur my vision. All I can think of is, somehow, relieving the horrible pain emanating from his grip. "No," I whimper. "Please. Please, let go."

Instead of letting go, he jerks my head to the side so he can hiss in my ear, "I don't like having things thrown at me."

"I won't do it again. I swear! I'm sorry. I—"

My plea is cut off as Stonehart releases me. My knees give out. I crumple to the floor and start to weep in a horrible mix of relief and humiliation.

"Lilly, Lilly, Lilly," Stonehart intones. I can feel him walking circles around me, like a lion around its wounded prey. "What *are* we going to do with you?"

I curl into a tiny ball on my side. My hands cover my head. All I can do is sob and shake.

"Now. You're scared of me. I can see that." Stonehart's voice is cold as ice, and deathly calm. "You're frightened. You're thinking: *What is he going to do next?*"

I give an incoherent whimper.

Stonehart squats down in front of me. I open my eyes enough to see him rolling up his sleeves. "I'm not going to beat you, Lilly," he says. "That isn't my style. Besides—" he chuckles, "—what use are you to me bloody and bruised? I want you *fresh*, my dear."

Without warning his hands shoot out and pin my shoulders to the floor. He swings one leg over me and shifts his entire weight onto my body.

His breathing becomes heavier. It's deep and raspy, coming from somewhere above me.

"Now." He sweeps my hair to one side to expose my face. "This little *adventure* of ours has got my blood boiling. I know of only one outlet for that."

I struggle against him, but it's no use. It's like trying to move a rock.

"Sweet Lilly." He caresses my cheek with the back of his hand. I can feel the hairs of his knuckles against my smooth skin. "Sweet, sweet Lilly. I must admit, I enjoy evoking such passion in you. But you must let me make an equal to it."

He lowers his head to my ear and adds in a heated whisper, "Fight back. The struggle… it turns me on."

Chapter Eight

I gasp as he grabs my dress with both hands and rips it down the middle. My breasts heave out.

"Yes," he growls. I thrash on the floor against him. "Yes. This is what I've been waiting for."

I try to scream, but the sound is muffled as Stonehart crashes his mouth over mine. The kiss is hard and brutal. I clamp my lips shut, but his tongue finds a way in anyway. I shake my head back and forth, screaming, *'No, no, no!'* in my mind. But I can't do anything against the assault.

One of his hands finds my breast. He grabs it and presses down hard, squeezing at the same time. Still I continue to fight, struggling beneath him like a pinned gazelle.

Stonehart pulls up from my mouth. His heavy breathing is almost feral, and it matches my own. I see pure, animal aggression in his eyes.

"Squirm," he rasps in my ear. "Kick. Scream. *Bite.* I like it rough."

I acquiesce his request by bashing my forehead into his jaw.

For a moment, he is too stunned to move. His grip lets

go. I squander my opportunity to escape by hesitating for too long.

Half a heartbeat later, Stonehart's hand whips forward and catches my neck. I gasp, feeling the blood being cut off from my brain immediately.

"So you manage to follow directions, for once," he enunciates, cracking his neck to one side. "That's good, Lilly. But you have to remember: I am *always* in control."

He releases my throat and blood swells into my head like water from an opened flood gate. The euphoria of oxygen reaching my brain again overwhelms me, and I drift into a momentary stupor.

Stonehart wastes no time. He takes advantage of my condition by flipping me over so that my face is pressed against the floor. His grip on my shoulders forces me down. I can feel the unforgiving marble pressing into my cheekbone. No matter how much I writhe, I can't budge so much as an inch.

I hear the sound of his belt being unbuckled, and then I hear it slide out of its loops. Stonehart grabs one of my hands and twists it back in a horrible, unnatural position. Pain shoots through my shoulder, and I scream.

I feel a leather loop tighten around my wrist. Before I

know what's happening, my other arm is twisted back in the same fashion. Both shoulders burn as if pierced by a molten spike. I thrash side to side, but the more I move, the worse the pain gets.

I give up and stop fighting. As soon as I do, and let my body go limp on the floor, the pain lessens. It's not gone, of course, but it feels markedly better.

Stonehart's breaths are coming heavy above me. I feel his weight lift off for a bare second. I don't try to take advantage. There is nowhere to run.

All of a sudden, I feel my dress being lifted. Stonehart makes a primal sound of satisfaction as air rushes over my ass cheeks. He slaps me once, not hard, but the sound of skin-on-skin contact echoes through the room. He chuckles, and then does it again, to my other cheek.

He stands up. "I like you like this, Lilly. You become very... *compliant*."

Out of nowhere, he hits me with a full-arm slap that contains enough force to make me slide forward on the floor. I cry out in pain. I don't even have time to brace myself before he does it again. And again. And again.

Each violent spank rocks my whole body. I don't know how long it lasts. By the time he's done, I don't even feel the individual slaps anymore. All my nerves are numb.

"Get up," he commands. When I'm too slow to respond, the command becomes an enraged yell. "I said, get up!"

I scramble to my feet, losing my balance twice in the process. My face is wet with tears and saliva. Stonehart grabs the belt holding my arms back and pushes me toward the table.

My whole body is shaking. I can't stop my tears. My former resolve? Gone. I just want out of this horrible nightmare.

"Get on," he says. I start to turn my head back, just to get a look at him, but he prevents that from happening by shoving me forward. I stumble and fall. "Goddammit, Lilly," Stonehart roars, "GET ON THE FUCKING TABLE!"

The rage in his voice makes me comply in sheer terror.

I struggle up again. Stonehart grabs the belt and guides me to our dinner table. With a broad, impatient sweep of his arm, he clears the dishware. Everything crashes to the floor.

I catch a quick glimpse of his face. It fills me with absolute, soul-wrenching fear.

It's insane the things your mind picks up in desperate situations. I feel suddenly glad that he hasn't made me face him.

"Lean over," Stonehart commands. "Face down. Breasts on the table top. Don't make me ask twice, Lilly."

I do as he says without a second's hesitation.

"Now," he continues, "Spread your legs. Stick your ass out. *Yes*." The word is a deep rasp. "God, yes. Just like that."

He steps up to me. I can feel the fabric of his pants brushing against my bare legs. His hands stroke my hair, then move slowly down my back. Down my back, over my ass, and—I gasp—right inside me.

"You're wet," he says. He can't hide his surprise. "Holy shit." His fingers start probing me. He chuckles. "Holy shit, Lilly, look at you. You might just be enjoying this as much as I am."

Somehow, I severely doubt that.

I gasp again as three of his fingers plunge all the way into me. He leans down and whispers in my ear. "I'm going to fuck you now. I want you to scream." His teeth scrape my earlobe. "Scream for me, little flower. Scream *loud*."

Chapter Nine

I lie on the table and cry out as Stonehart pounds into me. He's relentless, ruthless. I have no idea how long this has been going on anymore.

My shoulders scream in pain as he holds my arms back and drives into me, again and again and again, with all the fury and rage that I incited.

He grabs my hair and pulls me back, pressing down on my spine at the same time so that my body forms a half-moon arc. Tears stain my face as he starts moving faster, each determined thrust tearing into me. I can't believe his stamina. I curse myself for ever complaining about my ex-boyfriend's. There's karma for you.

The assault is endless. Try as I will to ease the discomfort by making my body relax, it's impossible. Every fiber of my being is clenched tight against the onslaught. It makes the pain worse.

Stonehart's hand darts around and grabs one of my breasts. In a quick, rough motion, he pulls out and spins me around. The back of my head bangs off the table. Stonehart emits a wordless, guttural growl and shoots all over my body.

Some of his cum gets on my face. I cringe and wince away.

There is almost no down-time as he pushes into me again, hard as a rock. I open my eyes and gasp at him. How is this even possible? He starts pumping his hips once more, both his hands grabbing and tearing into my body. He's panting. I'm panting, too. I force my eyes to the high ceiling overhead so I don't see his face. I close my eyes, and pray for this to be over soon.

***

Stonehart leaves me shaking and whimpering on the table. He does not say anything, or even acknowledge me after he climaxes for the second time. He simply unties my wrists and walks away.

I curl up into a small ball on the table top, cradling myself. My conscious mind flees into a dark, distant corner where nothing can touch it. It's a place where the pain does not feel so bad.

Exhausted, abused, and breaking, I succumb to a restless sleep.

Chapter Ten

I come to the next morning and feel warm sunshine on my face. I open my eyes. My head is groggy from nightmares. I discover that a thick wool blanket has been placed over my body.

I sit up on the table, clutching the fabric to my neck. I hold one hand to my head. Every heartbeat sends a shooting pain across my temples. I desperately need some Advil.

As if my last thought was a spoken wish, Rose bustles into my line of sight, carrying a tall glass of water and a little tray of pills.

"Here, dear. Have these," she says in her gentle, motherly voice. I take the glass from her with trembling hands and swallow the pills. As I do, she puts her arm around my shoulders and tenderly rubs my back.

Only after I've swallowed the pills do I realize that I don't even know what they were. Rose catches the aghast expression on my face and whispers, "Extra-strength Tylenols, Miss Ryder. And one morning-after pill."

The mention of *that* makes me suddenly sick.

She knows, I think in horror.

Of course she knows! My inner-dialogue counters. *She works for him, remember?*

"Come on, dear," Rose says. "I've set the bathwater hot, just how you like it. I'm going to help you get cleaned up."

I tug at the blanket. "You did this?" I ask, my voice small and weak. I hate how pathetic I sound.

"No, that was Mr. Stonehart. He came in this morning before leaving for work. He also left you this."

Rose reveals a small, velvet box. It's just like the one Stonehart gave me before.

"I don't want it," I say, bile building in my throat. "Please, put it away. I don't want to see it now."

"I'll leave it in your powder room," she says gently, before making it disappear in her pocket. "Come now, Miss Ryder, it's time to get you in your bath. I'll help you."

I lean on the graying woman's shoulders and let her lead me down the hall to the bathroom. I peek under the blanket as we walk and see that my dress is gone. *Did Stonehart do that this morning, too?*

Rose helps me step into the water. She makes no comment on the state of my body. The bath is blessedly hot, and scented with flowers.

"Let me wash your hair," she says after I've settled in. I

73

nod, still numb from the events of last night. "Lie back," she suggests. "Dip your head in."

I do. Submerging myself in the tub, I can almost forget where I am. *Almost*. The collar around my neck is a constant reminder.

Rose builds up a lather in my hair. Her fingers are soft and gentle. I try my best to relax, just a little bit.

A long time passes where neither of us speaks. After some of the warmth has seeped into my body, I break the silence in a small voice. "Why are you taking care of me this way?"

She clicks her tongue in a reprimanding but gentle way. "Mr. Stonehart asked me to look after you," she says. "But, that's not why I'm doing this. I'm doing it because I *want to*, Miss Ryder."

I look over my shoulder at her. She smiles at me, the lines of her face making her even more compassionate.

I wonder how a woman as kind and wonderful as Rose ever found herself working for a man as cruel as Stonehart.

"Thank you," I whisper.

"It's my pleasure," she says. "Now, I want you to close your eyes and relax. I promise, while I'm around, nothing bad will happen."

***

Rose cuddles me up in a fluffy robe and leads me from the bathroom. We enter the sunroom, and I discover that all evidence of last night is gone. The table, the cutlery, the broken dishware—all of it is gone.

In its place is a high-backed chair.

"I couldn't bear the thought of you sleeping on the floor," Rose whispers in my ear. "So I had the chair brought in. Mr. Stonehart may not give you a bed, but he said nothing about other types of furniture."

My heart swells with so much happiness and hope that I trip over my feet. Rose catches me before I can fall. She looks at me, concern glazing her eyes. "Miss Ryder? Are you all right?"

"Yes," I stammer. "Yes, I am." I feel tears building and can't do anything to stop them. I never used to cry so easily. I don't know what's gotten into me.

On impulse, I throw my arms around Rose's neck and squeeze her in a great big hug. She's blushing when I let go.

"Miss Ryder," she says clearly flustered, "I'm not sure if I deserve that."

"You're the first person to show me a sliver of kindness," I whisper. "Rose, you don't know how much that means to me."

She looks away for a second and fans her face. When she turns back, there are unshed tears in her eyes. "I didn't want to overstep myself," she admits, "…but, I had my suspicions." She takes my hand. "Come on. Let's get you dressed."

Chapter Eleven

Rose leaves after helping pick out my clothes. All I have for company is the dread of Stonehart's imminent return.

That, and the velvet box lying on the counter of the powder room.

I eye it without picking it up. I don't *want* his tokens. But my role—I shake my head—my role is to be his submissive. When my emotions get the better of me, like last night… bad things happen.

I need to be cold, dispassionate, and distant to have any chance of making an escape. I have to think like Stonehart. I have to *be* like Stonehart.

And I can't know what he's like if I stick my head in the sand.

My fingers tremble as I reach for the little box. I hesitate just before I touch it, then push through my discomfort and sweep it up.

It's heavier than the one before. I look over my shoulder to make sure I'm still alone. When that's confirmed, I push the lid open.

A small, folded sheet of paper obscures whatever is

underneath. I see Stonehart's handwriting on it. Revulsion builds in my throat, but I force it down. I take a deep breath, channeling my inner strength, and unfold the note.

Lilly,

For your cooperation last night, a second token. Their value is not in their worth, but in what they represent: Freedom.

Collect enough and they may be redeemed for a reward. How fast you earn them depends on your compliance. Once gifted, Tokens of Good Behavior cannot be taken away. They belong to you.

TGB Progression:

(5) earned to be allowed outside your rooms.

(10) to be given access to roam the estate, outdoors.

(15) access to newspapers to inform you of current events

(20) full internet access, with the caveat that your browsing will be monitored by me

(35) public outings by my side

(50) an early release from your contract

- J.S.

I stare at the last line of his note, hardly believing my eyes. He is offering me an *early release* with fifty tokens?

I know it's just his way of baiting me, giving me false hope. Hopelessness leads to despair. Too much hope leads to boldness. But hope, when present in just the right amount, can be a powerful motivator.

I tuck the note into my pocket but refuse to think about collecting fifty tokens. He's the one who gives them out. He's the one keeping track.

He will never let me reach fifty.

But the other milestones… I think he genuinely means for them to be accessible.

Three more and I'd be allowed out of these rooms? Hell, I'll take it. It's not the prospect of false freedom that excites me. Rather, it's the opportunity to explore his house.

It will be my first venture into gathering the information I need to get back at Stonehart… and ruin him.

***

The second token ends up being a heavy gold bracelet that I put on my wrist. I wonder if Stonehart expects me to wear all of them as I earn them. That sounds ridiculous, especially, when considering the higher numbers. My immediate goal is to get five.

Maybe fifteen.

I spend the rest of the day anxious on my new chair. All I can do is wait for Stonehart's return. Whether that happens tonight or tomorrow, I have every intention of being ready this time.

Chapter Twelve

I'm dozing off when the door to the sunroom slams shut. I jerk up, instantly awake, and find Stonehart glaring at me.

"How did you get that?" he demands, thrusting a finger at my chair. His eyes glow like embers in his skull.

I stand and face him. "Good evening, Jeremy," I say, keeping my voice pleasant.

He surprises me by walking over and backhanding me across the face. The force of the blow makes me fall to the floor.

"ANSWER ME!" he roars.

"Rose gave it to me," I mumble, cowering away. It's not like Stonehart *really* has any doubt who brought me the chair. Rose is the only person with access to my rooms.

Stonehart blinks. "Oh," he says, his rage fading. He stands straight and adjusts his suit. When he addresses me next, his voice is icy calm.

"Tell me, Lilly. Did you *ask* Rose for the chair?"

"No!" I gasp, clasping a hand over my mouth. The last thing I want is for Rose to get in trouble because of me.

"Hmm." He nods. "And you're telling the truth?"

I'm in too deep to back out now. I nod, eyeing him with caution.

"You know that I have every intention of finding out?" Stonehart poses. "If you lie to me, the consequences will not be pleasant, I promise that. I'll ask you one more time. Did you *ask* for the chair?"

"No," I say.

He smiles suddenly and offers me a hand. "Good! Then there's no problem here."

I hesitate before taking it. My cheek is stinging. It's probably already inflamed, but I won't give him the satisfaction of seeing my fear.

His strong fingers wrap around my small hand and he helps me up. When I'm standing straight, he takes in my dress.

"Very tasteful," he tells me. "Although a little wrinkled from your nap. Let's see…" he lifts the skirt up all the way to my waist. I fight the temptation to clutch the dress down. He takes in my bare legs. When his eyes focus on my exposed core, I can't help the little rush of heat that pools there. Holy shit, but that is *not* the reaction I should be having to him!

He lets my dress drop. "Nice," he says. "Very nice. Now,

82

do a little twirl for me, will you, Lilly-flower?"

I press my lips together and offer a tight smile, then spin once.

"Magnificent," Stonehart breathes. He picks up my left hand and fingers the bracelet. "I take it you received my note?"

"Yes," I say.

"Did you understand it?"

I nod. "Yes."

"Good. Because if you keep looking like this, I'll have no choice but to speed up the progression of your freedoms. I want you at my side. *Outside*."

My breath hitches at the suggestion. "I will do my best to earn the tokens," I say.

Stonehart smiles. "Excellent." He looks over his shoulder at the darkening sky outside. "It's a beautiful view, isn't it?"

"Yes," I say.

"Do you like it?"

I bite my lip to stop the truth from spilling out. In any other situation, I would love it, but I hate the view because of the false promise of freedom it provides.

"I do."

"I'm glad," he says. "Lilly, I'm going to be frank. I had a

long day at work. After our… escapades… last night, my mind was fixed on you the whole time I was there."

I swallow. "Oh?" My voice is small.

"Yes. The *courage* you showed facing me was extraordinary. Utterly brilliant."

I look at him without comprehension. "What?"

"I don't know," he continues, ignoring my question, "if one token was enough. I think you deserve more. Therefore—" he reaches into his coat pocket, "I would like to present you with three others."

My heart rises in my chest. Three means that I'll have *five*, which means I can redeem them for my first freedom! I feel moisture building behind my eyes and look away, ashamed to be crying. But they are joyful tears, a mixture of relief and disbelief.

"Lilly," Stonehart reminds me. I look at him, then down at his outstretched hand. In it is one beautiful, red masquerade mask complete with dazzling feathers. "Put this on."

My breath hitches. This is *one* thing. Was he lying? Was the promise of three tokens another trick?

"This isn't your TGB," he says, as if reading my mind. "But I do need you to put it on before I can show you what is."

I take the mask from him. Our fingers brush, and a jolt of electricity runs up my arm. I curse my weakness.

"Put it over your eyes," he whispers. He takes my shoulders and gently turns me around. "I will tie it."

I hold the mask over my face. Stonehart sweeps my hair aside, gentle as a zephyr, and ties the two strings. His hands run down my naked neck, skimming over the ever-present collar.

He brings his nose to my ear and takes a long, deep inhale. "You smell lovely," he says, his sexy voice rasping and doing all sorts of inappropriate things to my insides.

I have to fight his effect on me. How can my body *respond* to him this way? Rationally, it makes no sense. Just minutes ago, the man slapped me! Why does my reaction to him change so quickly?

He lets go, and immediately my skin tingles for his touch. I take a steadying breath and turn around. "How do I look?"

"Beautiful," he smiles. "Would you like to see?"

I don't have time to consider the offer as he takes out his phone and snaps a picture. It seems to please him.

"That," he says, turning the screen so I can see it, "is a dazzling woman."

I suck in a breath when I see the picture. My cheek is bright red and swollen from where he struck me.

I can't bear to see myself like that. "Please," I say to him, "put that away."

He frowns. "You do not think you're beautiful?" He keeps the phone directed at me.

"Jeremy, please," I beg. "Don't make me look."

"Oh," he says slowly, as if the realization had just started to dawn on him. "You're troubled by... *this*." He reaches out for my cheek. I flinch at the sting of his touch.

"Please, Jeremy."

"Very well." Stonehart pockets the phone. "A small imperfection only makes you more beautiful."

I feel an irresistible desire to scream at him, to tell him to stop the mocking compliments. Remembering where that type of behavior got me last night, I shove the urge down.

I don't speak, though. I'm afraid of what might come out if I open my mouth.

Stonehart motions to the chair. "Shall we?" he asks. He offers his elbow. I take it, and he leads me to the seat.

What this charade is, I haven't the faintest idea.

He lowers himself into the chair first. Then, he pats his lap. "Here, Lilly."

I can't disobey a direct order. I swallow and sit on his legs. He wraps his hands around my tiny waist.

"Relax," he whispers in my ear. "You're so tense. Your TGBs will be here soon."

I try to settle into him the way he wants. My body naturally wants to mold into his, and I fight the urge. Being around such a virile male makes me weak.

I hate that I cannot control that reaction. After everything he's put me through, and the promise of so much more to come, the only thing I *should* be feeling toward him is revulsion.

Yet somewhere deep down, in my very core, desire fights to come to life like a seedling searching for sunlight.

I stomp it down without mercy.

I feel Stonehart's phone buzz in his pocket. He shifts to take it out. "Ah," he announces. "They are here."

He taps the screen, and the lights in the room fade. The only one left is the spotlight shining on the pillar. It's a strange feeling to look at it from the outside.

"Jeremy," I ask, tensing up, "what's going on?"

"Don't worry, darling," he says. "I hired some entertainers for us tonight. *Three* of them."

Just then, baroque music starts to fill the room. It comes

from everywhere, giving the impression of being at a live orchestra. There must be speakers hidden in the ceiling and walls.

I hear the door behind us open. I crane my neck. The light from behind them illuminates two men, dressed in all black, rushing to fit a queen-sized frame through the door. I watch, a mixture of apprehension and curiosity building in my gut, as they run and place the frame on the floor directly beneath the spotlight. I sit up to get a better look, and Stonehart's hand tightens around my waist.

"Stay where you are," he warns.

I fall back. The two men return with a mattress, and put it on top of the frame. The music continues in the background. One of the men unravels a sheet, and the other darts away to bring in pillows. Soon, there is a beautiful, perfectly made bed in the center of the room.

"I know what you're thinking," Stonehart whispers, "and no, that bed is not for us. At least, not for tonight." He voice becomes an octave lower and a pitch deeper. "Instead of *us* fucking," he rasps in my ear, "I thought we could watch others do it."

"What?" I hiss.

"You heard me." Stonehart's hands press into the flesh

of my belly protectively. "Enjoy the show."

The music picks up. Three beautiful women trail in. Each is wearing a silk, sheer gown. The flowing garments differ only in color. One is red, the other violet, and the last blue.

The three women hold hands and run around us once, graceful as ballerinas. Their steps are timed to the music. They giggle and laugh as they throw ribbons of lace in the air.

Stonehart settles back, clearly comfortable. I sit on his lap strung tight as a violin string.

When one of the dancers makes her way to the bed, the others follow. She falls back, her dark hair spread around her head, and beckons the one in the blue to kiss her.

They start to make out, hot, sensual, and lusty. The third woman gently caresses their combined bodies.

Not half a minute later, I feel Stonehart's hand travel up my leg. I squirm and press my knees together, hoping to deter him.

"Lilly," he says in my ear, "the show is turning me on."

His low growl makes my clit throb. I shove the sensation away.

Stonehart is not a good man, I want to scream at my body. *Stop reacting to him!*

Thankfully, his hand does not go farther than my thigh. My eyes focus on the three lovers again. Their tops have come off, and they are consuming one another, absolutely uninhibited by being watched. There is something very subtle and sensual about the way their bodies come together. It is not crude and forced, but softer, more like art. More like... *real* lovemaking.

Another unconscious pulse of heat runs through me. I clear my throat to try to forget Stonehart's hand lying against my bare skin.

That only draws his attention back to me.

My breathing quickens as Stonehart forces his hand into the smooth recess between my thighs. Conflicting emotions rage through me: Revulsion at the way my body responds to him. Disgust with how weak he makes me. And, beneath it all, an undeniable current of *need*.

I try to ignore it all. I try to ignore the moaning that is filling the room. I try to pretend the steady fingers that are massaging me are not there.

But when the first ripple of pleasure spreads through my body, I can't help a sharp intake of breath. Stonehart makes a sound of amusement behind me, and redoubles his efforts. I shudder as another splash of pleasure rocks my body. I want to push his hand away, to stop the onslaught on my senses. But, I can't. I'm not *allowed* to fight him… not unless I want to evoke his wrath.

I dig my nails into the armrests, instead. His fingers keep moving, making my body thrum like a well-tuned harp. The darkness of the room and the performance before me does not let my mind focus on anything *but* sex. My heart beats faster, my breaths become rapid. I can feel my breasts becoming heavy and tender. I do everything I can to fight the visceral, animal reaction that Stonehart is evoking in me.

It's no use. I give another little gasp as one more wave of pleasure breaks through my defenses. The three women are now totally consumed in a powerful ménage a trois. Their cries and moans and all the slippery sounds of sex fill my ears, making it impossible *not* to feel turned on.

"You're close," Stonehart rasps. I bite my lip and give a muffled sob, shaking my head.

"You are. I can feel it." His free hand darts up and kneads my breast. The air leaves my lungs in a burst.

"Come for me, Lilly-flower," Stonehart says. "Come for me now!"

The command rips open the floodgates. I gasp as the enormous, built-up wave of arousal crashes into my body.

For a moment, I soar, lost in a sea of pure ecstasy, before coming back to earth.

Stonehart gives a shuddery moan and withdraws his fingers from between my legs. "Taste," he commands, bringing them to my lips.

I have no choice but to lick them, for the first time ever, tasting my own juices. Stonehart pulls his fingers out of my mouth and brings them to his own. His clasp loosens on my waist. I have no resistance left as my melted body sags into him.

Chapter Thirteen

I wake up late the next morning. I'm alone. There's a kink in my neck from falling asleep the wrong way in the chair.

Stonehart got up and walked out moments after he brought me to orgasm. I was left alone in that room, an uncomfortable spectator. The girls paid me absolutely no mind. When their games finally finished, they lounged on the bed in a sweet, unhurried embrace for a long time. I didn't dare stand or talk to them, even without Stonehart present. I did not want to break any of his rules.

At first, I wasn't sure how long they would be there. But eventually, they stood up, one by one, and filed out. I fell asleep in the chair soon after. Remembering Stonehart's reactions when he found me in it, I did not want to risk the bed.

I stretch and roll my shoulders, trying to loosen the tightness. The morning sun reflects off the glassy sea outside, bathing the sunroom in a cool, fresh light.

Excitement fills me as I stand up. The day is beautiful, and soon, I will be able to redeem my first freedom.

"Who are you, Stonehart?" I mumble under my breath. Today, I intend to find out.

I go to the breakfast room, where my food is already waiting for me. There is a folded note leaning against the plate.

I sit down and open it.

Lilly,

An unexpected business trip sent me away. I will be gone for three days. I have not forgotten about your reward. You will find the door before you unlocked. I have extended the collar's range. You are allowed anywhere in my home except my office. Rose will give you a tour.

Do not leave the house. You know what will happen if you disobey.

I hope you will give me no reason to regret my decision.

- J.S.

The note falls from my hand and I stand on unsteady legs, food forgotten.

The door is unlocked.

I walk up to it in a daze. My hand closes over the handle. I take a deep breath, and push down.

Disbelief fills me as I feel the handle shift beneath my fingers. The lock opens, and I push the door outward.

A long hallway stands before me, illuminated by soft lights running along the ceiling. The cinder block walls are painted an earthy brown. A lacquered red hardwood floor reflects the light.

I bring a shaky hand to my collar. This is it. When I take my first step, I'll know if Stonehart is playing another cruel game with me, or if he actually stands by his word.

Adrenaline pulses through my body as I inch my foot onto the hardwood floor. Carefully, I shift my weight onto it… and wait.

Nothing happens.

I steady myself against the doorway and pull myself through. I take a few careful steps forward, waiting for the telltale tingle under my ear.

Nothing.

Astounded, I continue walking. Slowly.

Stonehart told the truth.

With a pounding heart, I make my way down the hall. My hands are outstretched to either side of me, trailing along the walls. The feel of the coarse cement under my fingertips is electric.

I glance over my shoulder every few steps, hardly believing this is real, half expecting to be shocked at any moment.

At the end of the hallway is a set of grand oak doors. They remind me of the ones in Stonehart's office. The ones I saw more than six weeks ago.

Jesus Christ, I've been here for a long time. I stop for a moment and wonder if anybody in the outside world is thinking about me. Sonja and Fey must have heard that my internship fell through by now.

But then again, how would they? They likely think that I'm busy working. Hell, they're probably *happy* I haven't called them yet. It must mean that I'm so busy living my dream.

I give a sour chuckle. If they had any idea...

I open the final set of doors and come upon a magnificent lobby. No. Magnificent does not even begin to describe it. It's simply... sublime.

It's a circular space on the ground floor. High above me—higher even than the ceiling in the sunroom—hangs a pure crystal chandelier. I think it might be worth more than the entire building of my old Palo Alto apartment.

Stairs spiral around the outside of the room, leading to the second floor. To my left, enormous entrance doors are flanked by two skinny windows. I go up to one and look through it.

The air leaves my lungs in a gasp. The lawn in front extends as far as the eye can see. A driveway winds through it, splitting up into a roundabout before the mansion. A beautiful, white clay fountain depicting two angelic beings in a lover's embrace is in the middle, looming larger than life.

Tall spruce trees and evergreens stand on either side of the driveway like soldiers at the ready. I'm sure if I could see all the way to the end, there would be a massive iron gate.

Footsteps on the marble floor make me jump and turn around. My heart is beating out of my chest when my eyes fall on Rose, descending the stairway and smiling warmly at me.

I breathe a sigh of relief.

"Miss Ryder," she says, giving a little curtsy. "Mr. Stonehart told me to be expecting you today."

"Please, Rose, there's no need for formalities," I start. I cut off when I see her eyes dart above me. I follow her gaze, and find a camera pointed right at us.

Her eyes come back to me, holding warmth and kindness, but also caution. "Mr. Stonehart asked me to show you around the estate."

I clear my throat. "Yes," I say. "Please."

97

Rose gives an almost imperceptible wink and turns away. "Follow me."

As I trail after her through the rooms, I can't help but think of what an extravagant waste all this space is. Stonehart lives here alone. He must, for I haven't seen any hint of a woman's presence. Yes, I get that he's rich, but having so much square footage all to himself makes me uneasy.

Why does one person need so much space? What is he trying to prove? What is he trying to hide?

Other than you? a cynical voice asks me.

Every once in a while, Rose stops seemingly for no reason at all and glances back at me. Each time, a small gesture on her part alerts me to the presence of another camera. I get what she's doing, and couldn't be more thankful for it. Rose is reminding me that our entire interaction is being monitored by Stonehart.

"Does Mr. Stonehart entertain often?" I ask almost an hour later, when we return to the lobby.

"Oh, no," Rose shakes her head. "He never invites people here. He has an apartment in the city for that sort of thing."

"Does he spend a lot of time there?"

"Not since you came along," she tells me, and smiles.

"Miss Ryder, excuse my candor, but I really must tell you something."

"Go ahead," I say.

"Well, I don't know the particulars of your arrangement with Mr. Stonehart, and it's certainly not my place to ask, but I only want to say that since he welcomed you into his life, Mr. Stonehart has been a changed man. I have never seen him so content."

I frown, wondering if this is a test Stonehart told Rose to put me through. I remember the camera above me. "Thank you," I say noncommittally.

She nods at me in a way that I'm almost certain means, "Well done." She turns away.

"I'll be on my way, now," she says. "There's nothing more for me to show you."

"Where are you going?"

"Home."

My eyes widen. "You mean, you don't live here?"

"Heavens, no! I've always preferred my own bed. Especially when Mr. Stonehart isn't around to call on me."

"Okay," I say, processing this new information. Stonehart is trusting me to be *alone* in his entire house? This has got to be a trick. I need to proceed with caution.

"Charles—the cook—will be in shortly to make your dinner," Rose says. "You may introduce yourself if you'd like, but be warned: He is not very talkative."

"I will, Rose. Thank you for showing me around."

"It was my pleasure. Whatever makes Mr. Stonehart happy makes me happy, and *you* make him very happy." She walks by me through the door. "Good-bye."

After the doors close, I stand still for the longest time. The house is silent. The only thing I can hear is the blood pounding in my ears.

This has to be a test, I tell myself. *There is no way Rose has her own place.*

Stonehart wouldn't risk her finding out about me and raising an alarm. Things cannot be so simple.

A terrifying thought creeps into the depths of my mind. Stonehart would not risk Rose knowing about me… *unless she's in on it, too.*

That makes my skin crawl. Could kind, sweet Rose be involved in my capture? Could she and Stonehart *both* be in on it?

After thinking on it for a while, I see how that can totally make sense. What is Rose's *real* relationship with Stonehart?

I don't know. But, whatever it is, I intend to find out.

And until I do, I have to remember to stay on my guard around her—no matter how much that hurts me.

I have no friends here. To think otherwise would be lunacy.

It is a dark, depressing thought.

Chapter Fourteen

I walk through the entire mansion, not touching a thing, but imprinting the layout in my mind. Stonehart said he'd be gone for three days. I plan on making use of that time.

There is a pool, a bar, and a theater in the basement. The pool is a full, Olympic size one. I never really liked to swim, but my body is itching for physical exercise. Doing something strenuous can empty my mind. I make a note to check if my closet includes swimwear later tonight.

I look behind the bar, and find it stocked with all kinds of liquor. I debate pouring myself a glass—Stonehart never mentioned restrictions on consumption. Ultimately, I decide against it. Who knows if he'll take it as a transgression.

I return to the main floor and do a second walkthrough of the mansion. I'm looking for anything that will give me a clue about Stonehart, the person. If I'm to ferret out information I can use against him, that would be the best place to start.

Unfortunately, my search comes up empty. I'm not yet bold enough to open drawers and closed doors, but even if I were, I doubt I would find much. The house is sterile. It's decorated well, with modern furnishings accentuating the architecture. However, it feels more like a showroom than a *real* home. The few paintings on the walls are generic and nondescript. There is no clutter anywhere, and not even a hint of dust that could give me some clue about which rooms are used less than others.

Roaming around gives me no sense of Stonehart the *man*.

Eventually, I find my way to one of the living rooms. Two leather couches stand facing each other in front of a gas fireplace. I find the switch and turn it on. The flames come to life, dancing behind the glass. I sit down and watch them.

At exactly six o'clock, a bell chimes from down the hall. Curious—but cautious—I rise to see what it is. I walk into the kitchen, and discover a full meal laid out on the dining table.

There is no sign of Charles.

"Hello?" I call out. After Rose's warning, I've given little thought to the cook, but now seems like a good time to at least thank him. "Is anyone there?"

Silence.

Frowning, I sit down at the table, and discover another note.

Lilly,

I am pleased with your behavior thus far.

- J.S.

A floorboard creaks behind me. I whip my head around. There's nobody there.

I take a few deep breaths to slow my racing heart. How can Stonehart be "pleased" with my behavior if he's on a business trip? Rose pointed out the cameras for me, but surely Stonehart has more important matters to attend to than watching me.

Then again… I look at the note more closely. It's in the same blue ink as all the others have been. This isn't a message he faxed in.

The obvious answer is that he wrote it before he left and asked Charles to give it to me. Or, maybe he wrote *two*—one saying he's pleased, the other displeased—and depending on what Rose relayed, had Charles give me the appropriate one.

That makes the most sense. It also means that I passed whatever test Rose put me through. For a forgotten moment, I gloat in that feeling, pleased that I have done something right…

I come to myself with a violent shudder. I am *not* here to

be pleased that I have made Stonehart happy. At least, not *intrinsically*! It's all supposed to be an act.

Except… *what happens when the act becomes reality?*

Hunger gone, I push my food aside and stand up. Stonehart made mention of his office in the note this morning. Rose did not point it out to me during our tour. It may have been a simple oversight on her part. Yet I know that Stonehart's office is the one place in this whole mansion where I might find something that might help my quest.

I consult the blueprint of the estate I have built in my head. It's split into two massive wings, and the entrance foyer. There are three levels: the basement, the main floor, and the top floor. The sunroom is part of the west wing, facing the Pacific Ocean.

Out of nothing more than a desire to spend as little time as possible in that general area, I head east to renew my search.

I walk down the wide hall all alone, my feet making the only sound against the cold floor. I pass one empty room after another. Oh, they might have some furniture in them, but they *feel* empty. Empty, abandoned, and neglected. Like nobody even lives here.

My search on the main floor comes up empty. And I've

already been in the basement—more than once. I walk back to the foyer and climb the stairs.

I pause at the doorway of the master bedroom. It's the largest room in the house, larger than even the sunroom. It's constructed in a similar style. Floor-to-ceiling windows overlook the ocean. Rose kind of glazed over this room when we passed.

I stop and peer in, thinking hard. Stonehart said I couldn't go into his *office*. He made no mention of his bedroom.

Unless he considers his bedroom his office, I think to myself. I don't really believe that's the case, but I still proceed with caution.

I adjust the collar on my neck, give a quick prayer that I won't activate it, and step inside.

I squeeze my eyes shut and wait. When nothing happens, I open them slowly. A chill runs down my spine as I come to grips with the fact that I am in Stonehart's bedroom. I am actually *in* his bedroom. I wonder how many other women have been here.

I take a little step forward, still straining to feel the quick warning jolt that my collar gives me. My stomach heaves as I remember the agony that I experienced when I wandered over my boundary that first day.

One step, wait. One step, wait. I proceed like that all the way to the glass wall. When I'm finally there, I exhale a sigh of relief. Stonehart didn't lie: I really *am* allowed through any unlocked door.

I look behind me at the bed. It's the biggest I've ever seen, at least twice the size of a California King. Why does a single man need so much space?

But everything about Stonehart is larger than life. He told me that he is a man who *can*, so he *does*. I guess all of this— the mansion, the bed, the vast display of wealth—is the manifestation of that.

I walk up to the bed so close my shins almost touch it. I feel like I'm impinging on a sacred space. I reach down to feel the black covers, and then stop short.

It really feels like I'm intruding. I do not want to do anything to make Stonehart mad.

Just then, out of the corner of my eye, I notice movement against one wall. I spin toward it—but there's nothing there.

Strange, I think. It must be my nerves playing tricks on me. Feeling decidedly discomfited, I start for the door...

And stop again when I feel a tiny breeze blow against my

107

face. The windows are all closed. Where did the draft come from?

I look back at the wall, and that's when I see it: a tiny crack running vertically that looks suspiciously like the outline of a door.

Looking around to make sure I'm still alone, I tiptoe toward it cautiously. When I'm standing right by it, I can see that *yes*, it definitely *is* a hidden doorway.

Against my better judgment, and with my heart pounding hard, I push it forward.

The door opens.

The room is dark. The only thing illuminating it is a series of black television screens on the opposite wall. There are dozens of them, almost like an electronics shop. There is no video feed, but the screens are on nonetheless.

An uncomfortable twisting sensation rises in my stomach. It is a lot like anxiety. I don't think I'm supposed to be in this room.

But, I am not breaking any of Stonehart's rules. He said I could walk through any unlocked doors. This one was definitely not locked.

Curiosity propels me forward. The first step I take is small. If I were really not allowed in here, the collar would alert me to it.

I tense and wait for the warning shock. This must be the hundredth time I've expected it today. I still can't fully come to grips with the fact that I am free to wander through Stonehart's house.

There is a desk in the center of the room that looks like a command console. I see a wireless keyboard and mouse combo on the lacquered surface. There is a chair behind it, facing the wall of screens.

This is the first room that I think might actually contain something that will help me in my quest. There was no sign of electronics in other parts of the house.

My heart lurches as I take my second step past the door. A terrifying thought comes to me: *What if this is Stonehart's office?*

He expressly forbade me from going inside. If this room is it, then I am disobeying a direct order.

I look around me again. Maybe I should just back out and forget I even found it? That would be the safe bet…

But, no, I can't. It's beyond time for some boldness. Stonehart wants me to be meek and broken. That only applies when he's around. The *threat* of his presence should not stop me. I need to exercise some degree of audacity if I have any hope of remaining sane.

I can't very well protest when he's around, but with him gone for three days, I can. I *need* to do something that proves to myself that I am not weak.

Besides, why would he make *this* dark place his office? It's small and cramped. There are no windows. It feels more like a cupboard than a real room, especially when compared to the extravagance of the rest of his house.

That seals my decision. I did not get instructions not to *touch* anything.

I walk over to the desk and lower myself to the chair. My heart is beating so fast I'm afraid it will burst out of my chest. My hand shakes as I bring it over the mouse and push slightly.

All of a sudden, images fill the screens. It takes me a moment to understand what I'm looking at. When I do, a sense of vertigo hits me.

They are the feeds from all the security cameras in the house.

I see the spots Rose pointed out to me: the foyer, the multiple hallways, the kitchen. But, I also see some I didn't know existed. There are six views of the sunroom. Four of my bathroom—including one right above the tub. I see my powder room from an unfamiliar angle. It takes me a moment to understand that the camera is *behind* the mirror.

A feeling of nausea overtakes me. I know that Stonehart controls all aspects of my life here—but I didn't know just how thoroughly positioned the cameras are. There's not an inch of unmonitored space anywhere in my prison. That means this whole time—the entire time I've been here—Stonehart has been monitoring my every move.

Revulsion and disgust rise in my chest. I push away from the desk. Not only have I been a prisoner, but I've also been on *display*, like some circus freak. My eyes dart to the screen showing my closet. He's seen me changing. I look at the one depicting my pillar. He's seen me crying. The displays shine menacingly at me. He's seen *everything*.

My head begins to spin. I need to get away. I start to stand, when a cold voice stops me.

"Lilly."

I freeze on the spot. All my muscles tighten in dread.

I turn around, dazed, like in a dream, and find Stonehart glowering at me from the doorway.

I'm too shocked for words. What is *he* doing here? He's supposed to be away!

"Hello, Lilly," he says. He looks me over. "It's customary

to respond to a greeting, you know."

"H-hello," I stammer. Stonehart's voice is calm, but his eyes betray the danger lurking under the surface.

Stupid, stupid, stupid! I berate myself. I should never have come in here. Now that he's caught me, I can't begin to imagine what he's going to do.

Stonehart walks into the room. He advances on me. I'm too frightened to move. My feet seem rooted to the floor.

His menacing scowl is too much for me to take. I avert my eyes and look straight down.

He stops in front of me. I can see the toes of his shoes. Black, sleek loafers with thin leather laces. Regular shoes. Normal shoes. Not the shoes of a maniac—

He touches my chin and lifts my head up. My breath hitches as I meet his eyes.

He looks at me for a long moment. I want to recoil from his touch, but I'm afraid that will only make everything worse.

"You're trembling," he observes. His voice is flat. "How come?"

"I-I don't know," I say.

He makes a displeased sound in his throat. "Don't lie to me, Lilly."

I swallow and look away. He jerks my head back.

"Are you scared?" he asks. I'd expect to find a hint of triumph in his voice, but I don't. It's as flat and emotionless as ever.

His eyes, on the other hand... there is a storm brewing behind those eyes that rivals the strongest winter gale.

My throat is too constricted for me to speak. I manage to nod, almost imperceptibly, while doing all I can to avoid meeting his gaze.

"Why?" he asks. His fingers tighten on my chin. "No lies this time, Lilly."

"Y-y-your office," I whimper. I sneak a peek around the room. "I'm in your office."

Stonehart nods. A bloodless smile curls his lips. It is almost a sneer. "And you know you are not permitted in my office, don't you?"

I close my eyes as a single tear leaks down. This is confirmation of my worst fear.

"Yes," I breathe.

Stonehart lets me go. I brace myself for the oncoming slap... but it never comes.

Instead, I feel him turn away.

I crack open one eye. Stonehart's back is to me. His

hands are clasped together. He is looking at the monitors.

"You knew the rule about entering my office," he says, "and yet, here you are." He speaks without looking at me. "Please, Lilly, help me reconcile that disparity."

I open my other eye. I'm still shaking. I feel like I'm standing in the middle of a frozen lake, right where the ice is thinnest. One wrong move, one improper word, and the cracks splintering beneath me will break.

"I can't," I whisper.

This time, Stonehart definitely sneers. "You can't," he repeats. "In that case, you have every right to feel scared, don't you?" He turns around. His cruel eyes shine in the dark. "Since you disobeyed my rules."

I try to swallow the enormous lump that's taken up residence in my throat. I'm screwed. My fight-or-flight response has definitely gone haywire. I can't fight *or* flight. I'm simply glued to the spot, utterly incapable of action.

I remember Stonehart's words, warning me of what would happen if I broke his rules:

I will leave you in the dark.

I can't—I *can't* go there again. I *can't* spend any more time chained to the pillar with an invisible leash. I *can't* face the oppressing darkness a second time. I can't. I just can't!

"Of course," Stonehart notes, turning on his heels and facing me with a victorious air, "There is one other possibility."

I just look at him, not daring to speak.

"And that possibility, Lilly, is this." He walks to me. I squeeze my eyes shut. He leans down, brushes my hair aside, and whispers in my ear, "This isn't my office."

A great wave of relief crashes over me. It breaks the stiff fear holding me up. I collapse into the chair.

Stonehart turns away and begins pacing in front of the screens. "Nevertheless," he continues, "your guilty behavior tells me you would have gone behind my back and broken my rules when you thought I wasn't present."

"I—no, Jeremy, I wouldn't—" I stammer.

"Quiet!" he snaps. "I don't want to hear your moaning. The fact is: You *knew* you were forbidden from entering my office, and I find you here anyway, in what you *thought* was my office." He glances at me. "That is almost as bad as the real thing."

I shake my head, but no words come out.

"The question is," he continues. "What am I going to do with you? I stuck to my word and gave you access to the estate. What do I find when I return? *You*, in the one place

115

you thought I had forbidden you from entering!"

"Jeremy, please," I start. "I didn't—I was only in here for a second. I didn't think… I didn't know…"

"That I would return to find you here?" He wheels around. "No. I can see how you wouldn't expect that. You think you're so smart, don't you? Sneaking around while I'm gone?"

"No, I promise. It wasn't anything like that…."

Stonehart cuts off my protest with a sharp gesture. "I think," he says slowly, "that it's time I tell you a little story, Lilly."

I inch back into the chair. He walks toward me and leans on the table. He crosses his legs and taps the desk with his fingers. "Where to start, where to start?" he says absently.

I watch him cautiously, unnerved by the very real possibility of an unpredictable reaction.

He spreads his arms and smiles all of a sudden. "I know!" he says, in an almost mocking manner. "Why don't I start at the *beginning*?"

I can hear the blood thundering in my ears as he looks at me, searching for a reply.

"Okay," I manage meekly.

"At the beginning," he repeats. "Well, this is how the

story begins, Lilly. Once, many years ago, there was a young boy. He had two older brothers, and a powerful father. He was smart, sharp, and ambitious. But, he possessed one great flaw." Stonehart's eyes shine at me. "Would you like to guess what that flaw was?"

I shake my head in response. "I-I don't know."

"He was born *last*," Stonehart says. His voice is soft and full of hate. "As the boy grew, he was passed over time and time again in favor of his brothers. Brothers who were slower, stupider, and less talented than he. But that made no difference to his father."

Stonehart pauses, waiting for my response. When none is forthcoming, he continues. "The boy's hatred festered. Only his mother saw him as a real person. The boy grew up and became a man. But, still, his father looked only upon his two brothers to continue the family legacy."

Stonehart's voice becomes deadly. "Do you know what happened in the end?"

I swallow and shake my head slightly. "What?"

"The little boy rose above all and *crushed* those who doubted him." Stonehart's forearms flex as he cracks his knuckles. "He learned the thrill of domination. More than that. Of *vengeance*." He underscores the word.

A heavy silence falls between us. I can feel Stonehart's eyes piercing into me. He's waiting for my response.

"What happened next?" I venture softly.

"The greatest day of that boy's life," Stonehart says. "Years later, he met his father in the courtroom to conclude a hostile takeover of his company. The boy had changed his name. His father had no idea who was behind it. And when father and son met... well, the triumph the boy felt was worth every struggle of his life."

"Why are you telling me this?" I whisper.

"Isn't it obvious?" Stonehart asks. "It's a warning, Lilly. You think I don't know what you're up to? You think I can't guess what you were looking for in here? I told you the boy had grown to like vengeance. Well..." he pushes off the table and towers over me, "...traits that are reflected in oneself are easily recognizable in others."

He knows, a small voice whispers in the back of my mind. *He knows I intend to deceive him. He knows I mean to fight.*

I suppress an uncomfortable shudder.

"Now." He turns away from me and leans over the desk. "Let's see what you were in here for, shall we?" His voice contains a dangerous quality.

"Jeremy, no," I protest weakly. "We don't have to do

118

that…" He ignores me and starts tapping the keyboard.

A few of the displays light up with what looks to be a surveillance program. Stonehart moves the mouse to the calendar and clicks a date in early October. "Now, how about this, hmm?"

My gut tightens in anxiety as I see myself lying on the floor by the pillar. The screen is green from the camera's night vision.

Stonehart looks back at me over his shoulder. "Your first day," he says to me.

He fast-forwards until I start to stir. My stomach begins to writhe uncomfortably.

"Jeremy, please," I beg. "We don't have to watch—"

"Oh, but we do," he interrupts. "Yes, we definitely do. Ah!" He stops the fast-forward and hits play. "My favorite part."

I watch, horrified, as I see the television version of myself venturing past the boundary. I see myself stop a few steps outside of it. I flinch in real life as I remember the sharp zap under my left ear. The Lilly on the screen tenses, then, after a few moments, starts to walk forward again.

I almost yell at her to stop. Dread builds inside as I see myself take careless steps toward the curtain. I'm going to get shocked… I'm going to get shocked…

Stonehart pauses the tape just as my collar is about to send me writhing to the floor. He looks at me.

"Do you remember what happens next?"

Unconsciously, I finger the collar that's so tight around my neck. "Jeremy, please…"

"This is why you're here," he says. "This is why you came into this room, isn't it? Now watch."

He presses *play*. I see myself collapse to the side and start thrashing on the ground. The video makes me relive all the horrible sensations. There's no sound, but I can remember the pathetic, high-pitched squeal I made just before passing out.

Stonehart is looking intently at me. I want to rip my eyes from the screen, but I can't. I know he wouldn't be pleased.

My nails dig into the palms of my hands as I watch the horrific movie. I'm panting. My heart is pounding as if I expect the collar to shock me at any moment.

Finally, the Lilly in the video goes limp. I tear my eyes away.

"Did you enjoy that?" Stonehart asks. "I've got a whole collection, you know. Let's see… what else might you be interested in? Oh." His eyebrows go up. "I know."

He turns his attention back to the surveillance software and starts searching for another date. This one is marked November 18th, 2013.

The monitors show me and him together in the sunroom. We're sitting at a table, having dinner.

I know what is going to come next.

I can't watch. I can't watch him rape me on the table top. It's too soon. The memory of that night is still fresh in my brain.

I need to get away.

I stand up. Stonehart notices.

"Sit down, Lilly," he growls, "Or you'll face worse consequences than a little video stream."

My eyes dart to the open doorway. My chest is heaving. I never thought I would want to be back in the sunroom. But now, I wish for nothing more.

"I said, sit down!" Stonehart yells.

I cast one last, despairing look at the doorway. I need to get out of here. But, the longer I remain standing, the worse Stonehart's anger is going to get.

Defeated, I plop back down on the seat.

He smiles. "Good. Now, watch."

My entire body is shaking as I watch the video start to

play.

"Wait," Stonehart adds maliciously. "I forgot to add *sound*."

He taps the keyboard, and, all of a sudden, our voices come from all around me:

'How was your day?' Stonehart asks on the video. There's a pause in which I don't answer, and then he says, *"You look surprised. Lilly, it's customary to reply to a polite inquiry at dinner.'*

'It was fine,' I sputter. *'How was yours?'*

Stonehart's expression changes to one of darkness. 'Need I remind you of our rules?'

I cringe as the conversation plays out. A dull throbbing starts up in the back of my head. Apprehension grows inside.

'…Of course I'm right,' Stonehart says. *'You'd be hard-pressed to find situations in which I'm not…'*

My heart rate ratchets up. My breaths come faster and faster. Real-life Stonehart is watching me, making sure I keep my attention on the screen.

Jeremy?' My voice shakes a little. 'May I ask you a question?'

He picks up the wineglass on the table and peers into it. 'Do you remember our rules?'

'Yes.'

My palms feel clammy. Sweat is trickling down my back. I feel trapped, with Stonehart's eyes on me. Cruel eyes. Monstrous eyes.

He knows what he is doing. He knows how hard this is to watch. And he's reveling in my discomfort.

'...Tell me what you need.'

'I need... air!'

I watch as Stonehart loops his arm around television Lilly's waist and starts to guide her outside. He looks so worried, so very compassionate...

'...My sweet Lilly, the moment I change the range, you will be the first to know...'

"Please," I beg. I can't bear to watch. "Please, Jeremy, turn it off."

"Off?" he frowns. "But this is my favorite part."

He increases the volume

I hear myself yelling. I watch as I stalk to the table and throw the wine bottle at his head. I see the flash of anger on his face just before he grabs me.

I can almost feel his hands on me again. I'm trembling. The sounds of the on-screen struggle fill my ears. He's grabbing my hair. I'm struggling against him.

I can't believe I'm being forced to live through this again.

I gasp onscreen and in real life as I see Stonehart rip my dress open. I feel light-headed and suddenly dizzy. I can feel Stonehart's eyes boring into me, watching for my reaction. I can see him on the screen, groping, touching me, dominating me with his powerful masculinity, and...

And it's too much. I cannot live through the moment again. My breathing is almost as fast as my heartbeat. I'm taking short little gasps. I'm vaguely aware they do not bring enough oxygen to my brain.

My eyes roll to the top of my head, my head lolls to one side, and I pass out.

Chapter Fifteen

I am having the most wonderful dream. I am back at Yale, surrounded by my friends. We're picnicking out on the grass. The late spring sun warms us.

Fey is sunbathing with her eyes closed. I'm lying on my front, pretending to read a book while sneaking glances at Robin and his friends throwing a Frisbee back and forth.

The gorgeous gothic architecture around me sparkles in the sun. I close my eyes and breathe deep, knowing that nothing can ever harm me here…

Suddenly, I'm falling through the ground. I open my mouth to scream, but the rush of air stifles any noise.

I land in a tight box. I scramble up, but as I do, the lid slams shut. With it, all the warmth of my body seeps away. I feel like I'm trapped in an ice cube.

I can't see anything. I reach out in front of me only to discover I can't move my hands. They're bound to my body by thick, heavy ropes.

It takes me a second to realize that no, I'm not bound by *ropes*. It's the body of a massive boa constrictor that has me trapped.

A scream forms in my throat. Before it can come, something tightens around my neck. I start to choke. It's another, smaller snake, coiling around my windpipe. It's black, almost like an eel, with red, evil eyes... though how I know that in the dark, I cannot say.

It tightens and tightens around my throat. I cannot breathe. I'm suffocating. I'm dying. I'm—

***

I come to with a gasp. My heart is racing and my shirt is drenched. It's dark.

I look around wildly and find that I'm back in the sunroom, on the unfamiliar bed. The heavy curtain across the glass wall is open, but it's night outside.

It takes me a second to see that I'm not alone in the room. Sitting in Rose's armchair, with his eyes on me, is Stonehart.

"So," he says. "Finally, you're up. I've been waiting to show you something."

He reaches inside his pocket. Takes out his phone. Swipes one finger across the screen.

Before I can blink, that evil, red ring of light is rushing

toward me from the outskirts of the room. I gasp and shy into myself. It stops in a tight circle around my bed. Pulsing. Threatening

"I want you to think, very carefully, Lilly, of how you've displeased me." Stonehart stands. "I wouldn't move from the bed, if I were you."

With that, he walks out of the room, shoulders back and head held high.

And I am left forgotten once more.

The End